THE
FIFTH SUN

K.S. Miranda

Trail Media
1320 Ynez Place 181306
Coronado, CA 92178
ChisholmTrailMedia.com
Facebook.com/TrailMediaLLC
Twitter: @TrailMediaLLC

Printed in the United States of America
ISBN-13: 978-0615832319 (Trail Media)
ISBN-10: 0615832318

Cover design and interior design:
Michael Manfredo of Freestar Designs

For Jeke Trimeni

"The sun, the moon, the stars are dazzled by your glow…"

PROLOGUE

The boy was exhausted as he carried his mother's favorite cocoa jug out of their adobe home. Only a year ago, his mother had spent hours lovingly molding it out of clay as if she were nurturing a newborn child. She had always been admired for her skill in creating unique pottery dishes, but this cocoa jug with its black serpent-like design, was one of her finest pieces. As the boy reached the stone wall that surrounded his home, he lifted the jug high over his head and threw it against the wall, smashing it into a hundred irreplaceable pieces.

"Thank you my son," said his mother with tears in her eyes. "I am ashamed to say that I could not have done that myself." She offered him a crisp, golden maize-cake and a gourd cup of cool water, which he accepted gratefully. He was quite hungry. He and his family had been working tirelessly for five days to empty their home of its possessions. While the boy ate, he became mesmerized watching his father and brother come out of his home laden with beautifully embroidered clothing, bed mats and other items which were destroyed and then added to the ever-increasing rubbish pile outside.

As the boy finished his meal, he called to his father, "Do you still need my help?" "Yes, my son," his father replied, "We must now remove the three sacred stones from the hearth and throw them away. However, they are heavy, so lift them carefully." The boy wiped the last crumbs from his mouth and followed his father and brother into their home for the last time. After properly disposing of the stones, the father carefully placed a wooden ladder against the home and held it fast. The boy's mother climbed up first, feeling slightly disoriented sitting on her flat roof with nothing to occupy her normally busy hands. The boy and his brother followed close behind.

Finally, after checking to make sure that all of the fires were extinguished, the father climbed up the ladder and sat next to his wife reaching for her hand. The boy looked up into the ever- darkening sky and waited to die.

****

The senior priests finished painting their bodies black, then tightly wound white loincloths through their legs and around their waists and began the long walk out of the city and up the distant hill close to Colhuacan. Upon their heads were placed high headdresses filled with the valuable turquoise quetzal feathers. As they ascended the hill, the sun was setting behind the snow-capped volcanoes, which ringed the valley, and the sky looked like the Emperor's artists had splashed their most vibrant paints across the sky in an effort to impress the Sun God himself. But the procession of men was oblivious to this breathtaking beauty.

When they finally reached the summit, the sun disappeared and the black-painted priests became one with the night. The men stood silently for many hours. A unique constellation of stars slowly appeared over the horizon. Suddenly, the high priest joyfully exclaimed, "O god of the Sun, lord of all creation, in whose hand lies the power of life and death over mortals, we humbly thank you that the end of the world is not now, that the movement of the heavens has not ceased and that this age will continue for at least another 52 years." He then whirled the holy fire drill, grinding it against a wooden fireboard. Faster and faster he spun, until a hot glowing coal appeared. The high priest feverishly tended and fed the uncertain flames until they became a blazing fire, for he knew that if the first new fire of the century went out, the Sun God would be displeased and night would prevail forever. As one of the priests approached the fire to light a torch, the flames continued to grow, and he felt as if he had descended into one of the nine levels of the underworld. He carried the torch carefully down the mountain to hundreds of warriors waiting with their bundles of sticks. One specially chosen warrior lit his bundle and raced toward the city below. His mission was to reach the massive limestone pyramid in the sacred precinct and climb over three hundred steps in order to bring this new fire to the Sun God's red temple resting on the top. The other warriors carefully lit their bundles and followed him down the hill to help re-light hearths throughout the Empire.

****

The boy's legs tingled as if spikes from a maguey plant were burrowing into his skin. He longed to stretch his legs out from their cross-legged position but feared the consequences of disobeying his father. No one had ever told him that his last day on earth would also be the longest. Just when he could bear it no longer, he was startled by a chorus of shouts ringing out from the neighboring rooftops of their calpulli. His father and older brother jumped to an upright position and threw their arms around each other. His mother grabbed his face in her careworn hands and turned it toward a hill in the distance. It was the strangest sight he had ever seen. Balls of fire were moving rapidly down the hill toward their city. The fireballs were being chased by the sun, which rose and grew with each passing moment. Frightened, the boy gripped his mother's hand, but when he saw the rapturous expression on her face he was confused. "Be thankful my son," she said, "The Sun God sent the priests a sign from the heavens. Our lord is allowing the sun to rise again. This world will continue. Rise and give thanks!"

The boy's father scrambled down the ladder and ran toward the approaching fireball. The boy quickly stood up, searching for his father, and his knees almost buckled beneath him from sitting for so long. As the fireball came closer the boy realized, to his relief, that it was actually a warrior bravely holding a bundle of fiery sticks. He was magnificently dressed like one of the gods that the boy's family worshipped. There was enthusiastic yelling as his father and the other men from their neighborhood struggled to be the first one to seize a burning stick and bring it to their homes. The boy saw some men get severely burned as they frantically grasped for the fiery brands, for if a man's hearth was not lit with the 'new fire' his household could be plagued with bad luck.

His brother grabbed him by the arm. "Come quickly!" he shouted, "We must find the hearth stones." As the sun rose higher in the sky, the boys clambered down the ladder and raced to the place where the sacred hearthstones had been thrown away not more than 24 hours ago. They carried the heavy stones into their empty home and laid them on the hearth just as their father stumbled into the courtyard, exhausted but exhilarated. He used the burning stick to light the new fire in their hearth as their mother sat on the ground with a lump of clay and joyfully began to create another cocoa jug.

CHAPTER ONE

Kan, the high priest, was meticulously sweeping the red-ochre temple. Although he had just begun to clean the sanctuary, the back of his plain black tunic was already soaking wet. Kan had climbed three flights of stone steps, 360 in all, to reach the top of the Great Pyramid, upon which rested the red and blue temples, dedicated to the Sun and Rain Gods.

Each week as he started to climb up the imposing stairs, Kan, who was no longer a young man, wished that he could delegate this job to one of the novice priests. However, maintenance of the temple was his duty, and he dared not risk offending the gods. Suddenly, a burst of flame appeared in the center of the room, jolting Kan from his thoughts. Fearful that he had somehow incurred the wrath of the mighty Sun God, he prostrated himself on the ground with his eyes tightly shut. "Arise you sniveling, cowardly excuse for a man!" commanded a booming voice, "Arise in the presence of the mighty Sun God, Huitzilopochtli!"

Kan struggled to his feet, trembling. He slowly opened one eye and gasped for air as he beheld the awesome sight before him. It was indeed Huitzilopochtli just as he had been described to Kan as a young boy. A gold headdress was wrapped around the Sun God's blue forehead. His arms and thighs were colored with blue stripes. In his left hand he held a burning serpent-like scepter, and in his right hand he held a wooden shield covered with one of the most intricate feather mosaics Kan had ever seen.

"O lord", cried Kan, "I was born in this age at this time to serve only you. It is my destiny. I have desperately tried to joyfully fulfill my priestly duties, and I pray to you unceasingly, but this is the first time you have appeared before me in all of my thirty-five years. If I have displeased you in any way please have pity on a mere, imperfect mortal..."

"Silence!" interrupted Huitzilopochtli, "You have no need for my pity, nor would I deign to give it to you. I have news for the Emperor and I have chosen you to be my messenger. Emperor Toltec and his wife, Mia, continue grieving for their three sons, all excellent warriors, recently killed in battle against our enemies. Mia is no longer of childbearing age, and they fear for the future of the Empire. But long ago, I made a covenant with the Aztec people that I would protect them and make their nation great. I never break a promise. Never. Therefore, you will tell Emperor Toltec that the Sun God has heard his pleas and that his wife, Mia, shall soon miraculously give birth. Her last-born son will inherit and expand the Empire. He shall be one of the most-revered Emperors of this Age!"

The Sun God glared down at Kan adding, "Waste no time in delivering this message!" Then, he swung his burning scepter over Kan's head. As Kan instinctively wrapped his arms around his face to shield it from the intense heat, he heard a hissing sound like a serpent poised to attack, then all was silent. He peeked out between his elbows; he was alone. Leaving the temple in disarray for the first time in his life, Kan hastened down the temple steps and rushed to the Emperor's palace, relieved to be, for once, the bearer of good news.

****

Eight months had passed since Kan had informed the Emperor of the Sun God's miraculous message. Mia was sitting in the palace gardens, her long, black hair plaited with precious jewels. She glanced down at her swollen belly and tears began to quietly drip onto her cotton blouse that was tied with a delicately embroidered yellow sash . "Oh Etta, it's been so long since I've felt movement in my womb."

"You look lovlier every day, Empress. Pregnancy suits you."

"I still can't believe that the Sun God has favored us by giving us this amazing gift. But I certainly don't feel lovely. I feel huge. I can't wait…"

Before she could finish, Mia doubled over in pain. "It looks like the wait is over, my child," murmured Etta as she helped Mia back inside the palace.

Etta knew of her reputation as the finest midwife in the Empire and felt it was deserved. Still, she was a little over-whelmed by the task before her: safely delivering the future king of the Aztec people. She carefully washed her old, wrinkled hands. Mia was so large and swollen it was hard to tell if the baby lay correctly or not.

Hours later, in the dark of the night, Mia was as pale as the limestone pyramid and her breathing was shallow. Etta prayed to Teteoinna, the patroness of midwives, for the baby to be born soon. As if in answer to her prayer, Mia suddenly screamed, "The baby is coming, Etta!" "You're doing so well," Etta coached, "Push hard one more time and soon this young warrior will be in your arms." Mia grunted and pushed although she knew from experience that the pain would be excruciating— she was not mistaken.

Etta eased the shoulders out, lifted up the beautiful baby boy, and placed him in Mia's pale arms. But there was too much blood. The old woman began to fiercely massage Mia's belly to staunch the flow that continued to pour onto the birthing mat. "Too much, too much," Etta quietly fretted. Mia wearily smiled, kissed her son's forehead, and lost consciousness.

CHAPTER TWO

The spotted jaguar moved stealthily through the forest. He hadn't eaten anything since the sun first rose in the sky; and now that its rays were warming the top of his black sleek coat he was hungry again. He walked purposefully through the trees towards the base of a snow-capped volcano. Soon he came to the edge of a clearing in which stood a humble grass hut and an adobe-brick shed that the big cat knew was filled with food. Jaguars are known for being able to move without making a sound; he took advantage of this skill now as he noiselessly entered the clearing.

****

Kneeling on the dirt floor of her windowless grass hut, Ama tirelessly moved her stone mano over the concave upper surface of her three-legged stone metate. Soon, the previously-cooked maize kernels were ground into a fine golden powder. She patted the powder into round cakes and placed them on a clay griddle over the open-hearth fire. While the maize cakes were cooking, she walked barefoot outside to get some beans from the food shed. The smell of cedar was strong as the sunlight shone through the tall trees nearby.

At the base of the volcano where Ama lived it was cooler than the city. It was also very isolated here in the woods and she preferred it that way. It wasn't that Ama disliked crowds, it was just that she had never become reconciled to the fact that she was unable to have children. When she had lived in the city, every new birth that she attended had been a painful reminder of what she would never experience. Moving far away seemed to be the best solution. Ama knew, of course, that many people were disappointed by her decision. Her reputation as the best sorceress in the Empire was well-deserved and people wanted her to be readily available when they needed her advice or a magic spell. Ama knew she had a certain obligation to the Aztec people to use the gifts the gods had so richly blessed her with. So, when other sorcerers' magic was ineffective she would return to Tenochtitlan with her leather pouch filled with herbs and special potions.

The last time she had made the trip, she was surprised to find that after a five year absence people still recognized her. Her long, thick black hair was now streaked with gray and a few more wrinkles embraced her eyes and mouth. But she was still a beautiful woman with high cheekbones, skin the color of creamy hot chocolatl and soft black eyes fringed with long dark lashes. Ama had never grown taller than her mother's shoulder but she appeared taller because she was so lean.

Suddenly, Ama was jolted from her daydreams by the strange feeling that something was watching her. She quickly turned her head, but saw nothing. She cautiously walked backward in the direction of the shed constantly scanning the surrounding area to find the source of her unease. With her sweaty palms extended behind her, she soon felt the shed door. As she turned to open it, a black shape exploded out of the forest to her right, crouched and leaped towards her before she had time to react.

The jaguar landed at her feet, placed its massive paws on her shoulders and licked her face. "Ollin!" she exclaimed as she began to laugh, "Why do you never tire of sneaking up on me? I'm tempted to cast a terrible spell on you." "I have yet to see you perform a wicked spell and I'm sure you wouldn't waste your first one on me" teased the jaguar Then it began to undulate back and forth, first slowly and rhythmically, then faster as if it were having an epileptic seizure. A fine white mist began to envelop the animal and then through the mist one could see that the animal's paws were becoming hands and feet. In fact, the whole animal was suddenly transformed into a man crouching on the dirt. The man waved his arms as if to ward off flies, and the mist dissipated.

"I have wonderful, miraculous news!" Ollin roared. His voice was always the last thing to return to normal. "We are going to have a son!" Ama took a step backwards as if someone had hit her. "Have you gone mad?" she gasped, "Why would you say such a thing? My womb is empty and it will remain so. It is my destiny and you know it." "My darling Ama," Ollin said as he picked her up in his strong arms and carried her into their hut, "Let me explain."

Knowing Ollin was starving, Ama placed a pile of warm maize-cakes and a cup of water in front of him and then begged him to tell his story.

****

"Initially," began Ollin, "It was a morning like any other. As soon as the Sun God lifted the sun over the horizon, I quickly ate and went outside to practice my spells and incantations. After causing various items to levitate and explode, I began to transform myself into an eagle. Becoming an eagle is so liberating because it is the only creature that can gaze directly into the sun. I feel omnipotent as I soar through the sky. As my body contorted spasmodically like a fish caught on a hook, I heard a low mellifluous voice callling my name. I peered through the white mist that was quickly enveloping my body, but could see nothing.

"After the transformation was complete and the mist faded

away, I flew above the treetops and with my now superior vision scanned the ground below, searching for the source of the noise. Suddenly, I could no longer see my shadow. I glanced up and was startled to see a huge grey cloud above me in an otherwise cloudless sky. As I tried to soar above this cloud it rose higher. In fact, no matter where I swerved, the cloud followed me as if we were attached. Then, without warning, raindrops burst from the cloud, drenching my feathers, making it hard to stay aloft.

"Finally, realizing I had no other choice, I dove down towards the forest. The rain turned to hail, pelting my back and stinging my eyes, making it hard to find a place to land safely. Off to my left I glimpsed a tree, taller than the others, which seemed to beckon me with its branches. Running out of options, as my feathers started to freeze, I flew to the tree and perched on a branch located halfway down its massive trunk. Instantly, the hail ceased but the cloud remained and the voice I had heard earlier thundered, 'Do not be afraid, Ollin. I am Tlaloc, the god of rain. My cerulean-blue temple is equalled in size only by the adjacent fiery temple of the Sun God. I merely stretch out my hand and rain falls from the heavens. True to my whimsical nature, I can bring flood or famine. But I am also the the god of fertility and today I bring good news. I command you to listen carefully to everything I say, for failure to follow my directions will result in the destruction of the Aztec nation as you know it.'

"The voice paused, then began again, 'Long ago, your ancestors searched for a prickly maguey plant with an eagle perched on top, by order of the Sun God. When they found it, they were commanded to call that place Tenochtitlan and build a city there, with the Sun God's promise to make their city great.

" 'This, as you know, has come to pass. The Aztecs have conquered other nations and Tenochtitlan is recognized as the supreme capital of the Empire.'

" ' I know all this my lord,' I interrupted.

" 'Silence, you impudent sorcerer,' Tlaloc bellowed. Then, he continued, 'The Emperor, Toltec, is wise and good but he is getting old and he has yet to name a successor to the throne since the untimely death of his three sons. But I tell you that the next Emperor has already been born and you have been chosen as his father.'

"I gasped and then quickly closed my beak.

" ' His fate was already determined when he was conceived and placed in the womb. Now it is up to you and your wife, Ama, to properly raise him to fulfill his destiny.'

"There was a long silence, then the Rain God gave me these final instructions in a voice so low I could barely hear him, 'Today, when the sun touches the top of the volcano, you shall travel south towards the southernmost causeway which leads to Tenochtitlan. As you approach Lake Texcoco and the entrance to the causeway, you shall see a massive maguey plant, taller than you are and wider than a canoe. Perched among the prickly leaves you will find a reed basket, and in that basket you will find a newborn babe. You shall call him Matzin. He is as precious as jade and must be treated accordingly.'

" 'I am honored my lord and unworthy to be chosen for such an awesome task,' I stammered, still stunned by what I had been told. 'And I will do everything in my limited power, both as a sorcerer and a man, to carry out your commands.'

" 'I would expect nothing less,' replied the voice haughtily. And with that, the cloud lifted high into the heavens until it disappeared altogether and the sun reappeared to dry my cold wings. I wasn't sure if I was capable of flying any further after this ordeal so I quickly transformed myself into a jaguar, climbed down the tree, and sprinted home to tell you the spectacular news." Ollin paused, trying to gauge Ama's reaction. "What do you think?" he asked gently.

"I think we should offer our thanks for this wondrous gift,"

Ama replied, her face streaked with tears. Then, she walked to the stone altar propped against the wall of their home and carefully lit the clay brazier in front of the stone replica of the Rain God, Tlaloc. Soon, the pungent smell of burning incense filled the room as Ama and Ollin bowed their heads in prayer.

CHAPTER THREE

Etta's clothes were drenched with sweat as she feverishly worked to staunch the flow of blood that continued to gush from Mia's inert body. One thing was clear. If Mia lived, she would have no more children. Suddenly, and inexplicably, Etta felt the muscles in Mia's belly contract. She glanced down and was startled to see the top of a head. "Oh my lord!" Etta exclaimed as she reached down to free the second baby's head. "Another boy, Mia" shouted the midwife jubilantly, momentarily forgetting Mia's unconscious state. Then, she screamed for Mia's maidservant to come care for the infant while she tried desperately to save Mia's life.

"Mia, your sons need a mother. Don't leave them now."

Mia could feel her life force leaving her body. She was deeply saddened that the gods had decided she should die. She longed to hold her beautiful new son in her arms but she was too weak and tired to even lift her fingers from the mat. She knew she should feel proud to die in childbirth; for it was considered a great honor equal to an elite warrior dying in battle. She would now dwell in the palace of the sun with other courageous men and women. But she was ashamed to admit that, given the choice, she would rather remain here on earth, watching her little boy grow into a fine warrior.

Then, from far away, she heard voices. One was her dear Etta sobbing and shouting at her to wake up. The other voice was not familiar to her but it was as soothing as a steam bath and she heard it whisper, "Return to the living my child. Your destiny has not yet been fulfilled." Mia, rejoicing, summoned all her remaining strength, opened her eyes, and said, "Let me see my son."

The old woman gasped and looked up from her ministrations when she heard the familiar voice. Mia's eyes were open and alert and the color was returning to her face.

In all her years as a midwife, Etta had never seen anyone lose so much blood and live. A mammoth offering to the gods was clearly in order. "My son," Mia repeated. Etta gently lifted the first-born son out of his reed basket and placed him in Mia's outstretched arms.

The baby immediately began to wail for food. As the child nursed, Mia said softly, "He is truly a gift from the high gods, from the place of duality atop the Thirteen Heavens. He is a strong boy and shall make a fine Emperor." Etta, momentarily stunned, said nothing. Did Kan not say that Mia's last-born son would inherit the throne? If that were true, the future king was not lying in his mother's grateful arms, but was being bathed and cared for by a lowly servant in a room at the end of the hall. Knowing that news of the twin would astonish Mia and possibly cause her already fragile health to be compromised, the midwife held her tongue, deciding to ask the Emperor for his counsel as soon as she could safely leave the birthing room.

When the baby had finished feeding, his long dark lashes closed over his dark brown eyes and Etta suggested that Mia rest also. Within minutes the room was peacefully quiet.

****

When Etta entered the throne room she was not surprised to see Kan, the high priest, there as well. Along the walls of the room hung many weapons of fine workmanship, including shields layered with brightly colored feathers, outlined in gold, and flint daggers. On top of a low wooden table, covered with a white tablecloth, were the remains of the midday meal, laid out on golden dishes. Two beautiful women, dressed in clean white skirts and sleeveless blouses were kneeling in front of the Emperor holding deep-finger bowls filled with scented water so that he could wash his hands. Two other equally beautiful women were holding out drying towels for him.

"Your service has greatly pleased me today" he said to them. "You may help yourself to the leftover food." The women bowed, expressing their thanks, then took the massive plates still laden with enough food to feed twice their number, and left the room. The Emperor sat back on his lavish throne with a satisfied smile. The throne was always disconcerting to Etta. It was upholstered with jaguar skin and the empty head of the jaguar rested on the top of the chair. The eyes had been filled in with many-sided mirrors so that it appeared to be peering right into your soul.

The Emperor, at last realizing the midwife had entered the room, leaped from his chair and strode towards her. She slowly bowed down as far as her arthritic bones would allow. "Rise and rejoice, Etta," Toltec exclaimed grabbing her by the arms. "The gods have truly blessed us, have they not? Two healthy, strong sons!"

"Yes, Sire," Etta replied. The old midwife realized by his tone that no one had told Toltec that he had nearly lost his beloved wife in the process. She saw no need to unnecessarily worry him now that the danger had passed.

"Has your high priest determined the signs of the babies yet?" asked Etta.

"Kan and I were just on our way to the ball court to do just that. Why don't you join us?" replied Toltec. They left the palace grounds and walked toward the massive stone structure inside of which the popular ball game, 'tlachtli', was played. They entered the stadium through an archway. Toltec was immediately assaulted by memories of his older sons playing this game brilliantly. He knew it was their destiny to die a warrior's death but how he wished he had been taken first so that he did not have to endure this perpetual ache in his heart. And yet, he reminded himself, the gods had miraculously blessed him, in his waning years, with two more sons. With this thought, he felt joyful for the first time in many years.

Etta also observed the court below as she slowly climbed down. She had not been inside the stadium for at least ten years. Nothing had changed except the increased pain in her knees as she navigated the steps. The court itself was long and narrow, approximately 4 rods wide and 20 rods long, big enough to accommodate over 2000 warriors Mounted vertically in the center of the longer side walls were small intricately carved stone rings. The game could either be played between two individuals or two teams. The two teams faced one another, one on each side of a central line. Either team immediately won if they managed to throw a rubber ball through one of the stone rings. But Etta had never seen a game won this way because it was nearly impossible to do. The rubber ball was almost as large as the opening in the stone ring, not to mention the fact that it was extremely heavy. And even though the players wore knee-caps, leather gloves and wide leather belts to blunt the impact of the ball, they often sustained severe bruising which led to internal bleeding and death. Etta was constantly amazed that the game remained so popular.

But they, of course, were not here to watch a ball game. In fact, it was eerily silent except for the sound of their sandals on the stairs. They finally reached the dirt court and walked towards one of the narrower walls, which was covered in black and red picture symbols. Toltec was still pleased that he had commissioned this massive depiction of the 'Tonalamatl,' the Book of Destinies. The high priest, of course, had the actual book in his quarters, but Toltec had always preferred to come to this larger-than-life reproduction to watch the high priest determine the destiny of one of his children after their birth.

Kan approached the painted wall. He was visibly nervous. Although he had performed this rite hundreds of times for others, it was intimidating to decipher the destiny of the Emperor's new sons, especially since the last-born twin would be the successor to the throne. Kan looked at the wall and forced himself to focus on the task at hand. The Book of Destinies delineated the 260-day ritual calendar. Each day was represented by a number and a sign, which, when interpreted together, conveyed an Aztec's future path. Only the high priest had the ability to do this. Kan found the previous day's number and sign and smiled with relief. "Your sons are truly honored by the gods Sire," he told the Emperor. "They share the birth sign '4-itzcuintli' which is one of the most favorable signs to be born under. This sign promises your sons success and prosperity. As young men they will be courageous and shine in war."

Toltec was overcome with joy. "Etta," he declared, "Prepare yourself for the naming ceremony—for it will take place tomorrow."

"Of course my lord," the old woman replied, turning to leave and then stopping short as she remembered something. "Most holy one," she said haltingly turning towards Kan, "The birth sign of which you spoke was for yesterday, was it not?"

"Of course, Etta. Was that not the day the twins were born?" Kan replied sarcastically.

"Well, yes and no...," responded Etta.

"I'm in no mood for riddles, Etta. What are you getting at?" said the Emperor impatiently, for he had other important business to attend to.

"Well, your majesty, one of your sons was born late last night and the other one was born early this morning," replied the midwife. "Therefore, we have yet to determine the birth sign of the last-born twin."

"Incredible!" Toltec remarked as Kan returned to the wall and then dropped to his knees in horror. "What's the matter Kan?" the Emperor exclaimed. Kan turned his head toward Toltec. His face was as white as a virgin's tunic and he was momentarily speechless.

"Speak up!" Toltec shouted.

Fearing the wrath of the Emperor if he remained silent, Kan swallowed the bile in his throat and said, "Sire, your fifth son was born under the sign '9-eecatl.' Kan paused then slowly added, "This is the most unfavorable sign of all. Your last-born son is destined to be a witch performing black magic. Death and hell will be his companions."

"Impossible!" exclaimed Toltec as Etta gasped unbelievingly. "What about the revelation regarding my last-born son? Is this some kind of cosmic joke on the part of the Sun God? Witches taking over an Empire that my ancestors and I have fought so hard to make great? I will not allow it!" roared the king.

Kan, fearful that the Emperor's anger would soon be directed toward him, racked his brain for a possible solution. Suddenly, he stood up and cried out, "Your majesty, I believe it is possible for the prophecy to be fulfilled by your fourth-born son."

"Go on", demanded Toltec.

"As you know, according to our ancient laws, anyone born under this sign must be brought to the witches' enclave, Malinalco, within three days after his or her birth. The infant must be left at the foot of the massive stone statue of the monster Tzitzi that guards the entrance to their city. Tzitzi then causes the baby's spirit to depart into the heavens and replaces it with a witch's dark spirit. The birth family mourns the death of their child and the witches rejoice at the addition to their coven."

"Perfect" interjected Etta. "Within three days, the son born under the favorable sign will be the last living son and, accordingly, the successor to your throne, my lord."

"Exactly," agreed Kan.

Toltec slowly sank down on one of the stone stadium benches and covered his face with his hands. This was not the response Kan was expecting or hoping for.

"What's troubling you, your Majesty?" Etta gently asked.

"Oh Etta, Mia and I were truly paralyzed with grief when we heard that our three older sons had been killed in battle. I thought Mia would never recover. But then, by the gods' wondrous design, she found herself with child again, at an age where most women are welcoming grandchildren. And the new life in her womb brought new life to our marriage. Etta, you know how dearly I love my wife. How can I now explain to her that one of our precious babies was born under such an evil sign that he must be taken from her and considered dead, to be spoken of no longer? I might as well pierce her heart with one of my arrows, for this news will have the same effect."

"You need not explain anything to Mia, my lord," Etta declared.

"I appreciate the offer Etta," replied Toltec wearily, "But this is something I must do myself, regardless of the consequences."

"You misunderstand me, Sire. You will not need to confront Mia with this horrific news because she believes that she gave birth to only one son."

"How is this possible?" exclaimed Toltec.

"There were some...complications during the delivery. Mia fell unconscious shortly after the first twin was born and did not regain consciousness until after the second-born child was carried away to be bathed by a servant. I did not want to overly excite her with the news until I was assured that her health would not be compromised. So, she believes that she has only one living son.

"Based on what we have just learned about the fifth son's fate, I see no need to tell her now. It would only wound her unnecessarily. The only people who know about the other baby are you, Kan, the servant girl and myself. I would suggest that you immediately transfer the servant to one of your faraway estates where her story will be treated as an unsubstantiated rumor by a disgruntled servant."

"What a remarkable turn of events," remarked the Emperor shaking his head in wonderment. "Your advice is wise, as always, my dear Etta, and shall be heeded. I shall take care of the servant girl. Kan, you take my 'deceased' son to Malinalco and Etta, prepare for the naming ceremony of my last living heir."

The high priest and the midwife left to perform their appointed tasks. Toltec waited until he was alone in the tomblike stadium and then his body convulsed with the sobs he had been suppressing. He felt like a sacrificial victim whose heart was being ripped out and offered to the gods. He clutched his body, fell to his knees and rocked back and forth moaning, wishing that this was a nightmare from which he would soon awaken.

CHAPTER FOUR

The little boy was watching his father light the resinous torches that provided a smoky light in their windowless home. His mother was weaving cotton cloth on her belt-loom, which fastened to her waist on one end and to a wooden post at the other. She was making a beautiful cloak for her son to wear when he left for school next year. Up until now, his parents had taught him at home, as was customary, but next year, he would enter the calmecac school, which was attached to his local temple.

He knew his parents hoped he would become a priest. He had been a sickly child and even now, at age 14, he was still thin, slight of build and nearsighted. Clearly not warrior material, his parents had admitted when they thought he wasn't listening. But becoming a priest was equally as honorable.

The little boy wanted to be a priest. First of all, it would please his parents, whom he dearly loved. But also, he was fascinated by the mysterious Book of Destinies that, when interpreted, determined an Aztec's chosen path. The high priest was the only one authorized to study this book and learn how to interpret the numbers and signs hidden within. What an awesome power and how intoxicating to be chosen to use it. If only priests didn't have to climb those hateful temple steps, the job would be perfect, he thought, for he had always been terrified of heights.

The boy's thoughts were interrupted by a sickly sweet stench coming from outside. His mother quickly detached herself from her loom while his father closed the door and moved their low table against it. Then, his father took a bucket of water and doused the fire in the big stone hearth. Steam began to fill the room, stinging the boy's eyes and making it hard to see.

"What's going on?" asked Kan waiting to be reassured that this was just some kind of drill with which he was not familiar. His mother put her finger to her lips, put her arm around his shoulder and quickly guided him toward the hearth.

"Please listen carefully to what I say," whispered his mother, "And obey me no matter what happens. Do you understand?" Kan nodded. " I want you to hide inside the hearth. No matter what you hear do not come out until this awful smell has gone." As he climbed inside the hearth, she followed him in and held him tightly. "I love you, my dear Kan. You are my most precious jewel. Never forget that." She started to walk out but Kan grabbed her skirt and pleaded, "Mother, please, tell me what is happening. You're frightening me." His mother turned and held his face and sternly whispered, "I have told you all you need to know. We have raised you to obey your elders and I expect you to do that unquestioningly now." And with that she walked toward her husband and held his hand as they stood silently against the back wall of the hut staring at the door.

The stench was now overpowering. Kan placed his hand over his nose and mouth as he peered through a chink in the stone. Then, black smoke started to seep in under the closed door. As Kan watched in amazement, the black smoke divided in half and sculpted itself into the forms of two large skunks. His parents stood completely stiff as if frozen. Before he could blink again, the skunks became real and he was paralyzed with fright. He knew that only witches could turn themselves into skunks. And unlike sorcerers, who used their magic for good, witches lived only to cause harm to mortals.

Just then the skunks' tails spewed out a horrible stench

*accompanied by more black smoke, which enveloped the animals'
bodies and then swirled up towards the ceiling of the hut, causing
a tornado-like wind which blew open the door and extinguished
all the torches. The soot from the hearth blew into Kan's eyes and
he was momentarily blinded. Through the loud rushing noise of
the manufactured wind Kan could hear eerie voices muttering
some sort of incantation. Then, silence.*

*He quickly rubbed the dirt from his eyes and when he was
able to look through the hole again, he stared in disbelief. The
hut was completely empty. He burst out of the hearth and ran
out the open door, searching frantically in all directions and
screaming his parents' names. It was no use; they had vanished.
He was alone.*

****

Kan, the high priest, woke up in a cold sweat, still screaming
his parents' names. How could something that had happened
more than 20 years ago still come back to haunt him in his sleep?
He slowly stood up, pulled on his long black tunic and combed
out his straight black hair that hung to his waist. Kan lived in
the priests' quarters, a large stone structure that was one of the
many buildings located in the main temple precinct. The precinct
was in the center of the city and was approximately 500 square
rods with a high stone wall surrounding it, which protected the
Great Temple and arsenals located within.

Kan watched the sun rise over the Sun God's sanctuary
and was thankful. For if it had risen over the Rain God's
temple there would have been inclement weather and what
he had to do now was hateful enough without having to
walk in the rain. He left his room, walked through one of
the three heavily guarded gates, and turned towards the
palace. As prearranged, Etta met Kan at the palace gates,

looked around to make sure they were alone, and then surreptitiously handed him a reed basket with a blanket covering its contents.

"I have given the baby a tincture of a special herbal potion that should keep him asleep for at least two hours. Plenty of time for you to reach Malinalco without arousing suspicions." Without waiting for a response, Etta turned and shuffled back into the palace with her head bowed, as if the weight of this task was too much for her to bear.

Kan walked through the city, clutching the basket, oblivious to the sights and sounds that assaulted his senses.

He passed through Teopan, one of the four quarters of the city outside the temple precinct. Whitewashed walls enclosed the homes of related families. Soon he reached the southernmost causeway. There were, in fact, three causeways, which had been built by the Aztecs to link their capital city with the rest of the Empire. This was necessary because the city of Tenochtitlan was located on a man-made island floating on the waters of the largest lake in Mexico, Lake Texcoco. The causeways were immense, more than three miles long and wide enough to accommodate ten horsemen riding abreast, if the Aztecs had had horses, which they didn't. Truly a testament to Aztec ingenuity and engineering, Kan recalled another priest saying.

The witches' enclave of Malinalco was located about two miles inland as soon as one crossed the southern causeway. Kan had two choices. He could either hire a laborer to take him across the lake in a canoe or he could walk. Kan clearly did not relish walking for more than three miles under the searing hot sun, but he knew it would be foolhardy to travel with a talkative stranger and risk discovery of the baby. So, he turned away from the many boatmen offering their services-for-hire and began the long journey south.

His tunic was drenched with sweat when he finally reached

the forested land on the other side. He sat for a moment on a rock at the edge of the lake. It was quiet here, for hardly anyone traveled on this causeway for fear of encountering a witch. The more he thought about his final destination, the more he trembled. Soon he was shaking so uncontrollably that he accidentally let go of the basket. It fell onto the thick grass. Kan quickly reached down and lifted up the blanket to make sure that the baby was all right.

The infant seemed to be sleeping peacefully but Kan was alarmed to see a small purple bruise on the baby's forearm that must have been caused by the fall. Kan knelt down to examine the arm more closely and realized the purplish marking was actually a birthmark. Ironically, the birthmark had an uncanny resemblance to the Aztec sign for "anointed one" or "blessed one." Kan couldn't think of any child who was less blessed than this one. Oh, how the gods toss us about and mock us! he thought.

He gently laid the blanket back over the sleeping child with his still trembling hand, then lifted the basket and continued on his way. Soon the forest became so dense that the sun had to fight to find an opening through the thick canopy of tall trees. Kan was alarmed by each noise he heard, imagining witches watching him from behind the branches.

Straight ahead was the immense statue of the monster Tzitzi that guarded the entrance to Malinalco. It was more horrifying than he could have ever imagined. It was at least three times his height. Its extremities seemed to be made entirely out of human bones. Its eyes were filled with large obsidian mirrors so that it seemed to be looking right at him. What at first glance appeared to be a feather headdress was actually a multitude of writhing, live serpents.

Kan was having trouble breathing, and his heart was beating too rapidly. Oh how he wished it would just stop beating altogether. Instant death would certainly be preferable to entering this hellish place. But the thought of the severe punishment which would await him if he returned with the baby caused him to slowly drag one foot in front of the other. Then, the tingling sensation that is triggered only by intense fear permeated his sweat-drenched body and he lost control of his bowels. The unmistakable stench of skunk assaulted his senses and the 20-year old memories exploded in his brain.

He turned and ran back through the forest toward the lake. Branches ripped into his uncovered arms and face as if trying to hold him back, but he felt nothing but terror. He was aware only of an overpowering need to escape this evil place. He soon reached the lake's edge. Still in a state of shock, he was amazed to find that he was still clutching the basket. Kan fell to his knees in despair. The Emperor would never forgive him for not following his orders. The punishment would be both harsh and immediate.

Then a vague memory seeped into his consciousness. Back when he was completing his studies at the calmecac school, one of his teachers taught a course on witches with the hope that if the students learned how witches operated they would be better equipped to protect themselves. He remembered that one of their rituals was to come to the lake's edge on certain inauspicious days, just after the sun sank below the earth, to collect juice from the largest of the maguey plants located here near the shore. To do this, the witches would slice the thick leaves with sharp obsidian knives, suck out the sweet juice and spit it into a gourd cup. These cups of juice would then be emptied into open vats located inside the enclave and left to ferment. The resulting brew was quite potent and could be deadly if ingested in large amounts. Today just happened to be one of the inauspicious days.

Kan stood up and looked around. There was no mistaking which plant the witches would gravitate towards. To his immediate right was a massive maguey plant at least twice his size and wider than the boats traveling on the lake. He approached it with the basket draped over his arm. Cautiously avoiding the spiky thorns, he set the basket in the middle of the plant. Less than 12 hours from now, the witches would arrive, the basket would be found and the child's destiny would be fulfilled. More importantly, the Emperor's command would be obeyed, albeit in a roundabout way.

Kan started down the causeway, relieved to have escaped the witches' grasp one more time.

When he returned to his quarters he was starving. The other priests were already gone performing their respective duties. On his way to the communal dining room he passed through the library. The Book of Destinies, which he alone could decipher, was kept here on a low wooden table in the middle of the room.

Reliving the day's unbelievable events, Kan walked toward the book and flipped to the page delineating the numbers and signs for the current month, the older twin's birthday being '4-itzcu-intli' and the younger twin's birthday being.... "Not possible!" screamed Kan as he yanked the book toward his face, looked again and moaned. The number and sign for the younger twin's date of birth was not '9-eecatl' but '4-acatl' and the difference was significant. Anyone born under the latter sign would be a born leader, courageous and just. How could he have made such a devastating mistake? Had the scribes incorrectly transferred the glyphs in the actual book to the ball court wall?

Frantically, he raced out the door until he reached the ball court. He raced down the stairs as fast as his old legs could take him until he stood directly in front of the wall. At least he was not crazy. The evil sign of '9-eecatl' was clearly written here. He turned around and sank down against the wall. He had no choice; he would have to recover the baby immediately. He would take care of the infernal scribes when he returned.

He rose to his feet, brushed the dirt from the back of his tunic and took one last look at the wall. Then he paused and took a closer look hoping he was imagining things. Yesterday's sign now correctly read '4-acatl'. Apparently the accumulation of dirt on the wall over time had made the '4' look like a '9' and the 'a' look like 'ee,' especially to a nearsighted idiot like himself. Rubbing his tunic against the wall just now had dislodged the dirt and revealed the true sign. He leaned over and vomited.

Due to his unforgivable mistake, the last-born son and true successor to the throne was lying in a maguey plant and would be abducted by witches at sundown. He must hurry. Faint from a combination of hunger, exhaustion and stress, Kan forced himself to walk quickly through the city. He dared not run for fear of arousing suspicion. Again he walked along the southern causeway until he reached the maguey plant. He carefully parted the leaves and gasped in disbelief. This time his eyes were not playing tricks on him. The basket was gone.

CHAPTER FIVE

The baby was just starting to stir. His light-brown eyelashes fluttered open and he started to cry. Ama gently lifted him out of the basket and held him against her chest with one hand while she picked up a warm bowl of milk with the other. She repeatedly dipped her fingers in the bowl and then placed them in the baby's mouth until he seemed full.

"My, you're a hungry boy," she murmured. She cradled her son in her arms and gazed adoringly at him. He stared back at her with his large, trusting hazel eyes as if he knew he was in a safe, loving place, which he was.

"Oh Ollin," Ama sighed contentedly, "He's perfect, isn't he?"

"Yes, my love. He's been in our home for only three days and I already can't imagine life without him."

Ollin was still amazed that the journey to and from the maguey plant had been so uneventful. The Rain God had clearly been protecting them from harm as they traveled near the witches' territory. He stroked the baby's cheek, marveling that anything could feel so soft. The baby reached up and grabbed Ollin's finger with his soft pudgy hand and Ollin laughed.

"He already has a strong grip. A good sign for a future warrior."

Ama lightly ran her fingers over the small purplish birthmark on the baby's forearm. "I am even thankful for this discoloration on his skin," Ama admitted, and Ollin, understanding her meaning said, "As am I." For the Aztecs nourished the Sun God daily with sacrificial blood. Generally, the victims were prisoners of war. But on one day each year the victim had to be an Aztec man or woman with no physical imperfections. Thankfully, their son would be spared that fate.

Ama carried the baby outside where earlier Ollin had placed a small earthen tub of water. The baby's eyes immediately closed tightly against the bright sunlight. Ollin placed a miniature bow, arrow and shield in the infant's hand and the baby instinctively wrapped his fingers around it. Ollin had spent days carving these small items so that they would be ready for the naming ceremony today.

Ama bathed the baby in the tepid water and then held him up toward the heavens saying, "Dear son, you are a precious stone, a true gift from the gods. Although you were not born in this house, it is now your nest, your place of comfort and safety and unconditional love. We love you more than life itself. But at some point baby birds must grow and leave the nest and we will do everything in our power, with the divine help of all the gods in the heavens, to prepare you for your future role in the Aztec Empire. For you, my son, will be a leader among men, revered throughout the ages."

Ollin then dipped his fingers in the water and set some drops in the baby's mouth saying, "Take and receive this, for it is with this heavenly water that you will live upon the earth and grow. These waters will wash and purify your heart. Wherever you may be, oh evil ones, you who might do this child mischief, leave him, go away. He is protected now."

Then, Ama presented the child four times to the heavens and said joyfully, "We present to you our beloved son, Matzin." Ama and Ollin both kissed the baby's forehead. Then, Matzin, who had been unbelievably quiet throughout the whole ceremony, suddenly let out a yelp. He was hungry again.

Many miles away, in the palace courtyard, another baby was being named. But this ceremony was much more elaborate, as befitted an Emperor's son. The past two days, the servants had worked at a feverish pace to prepare the food and drink for the feast that would follow the ceremony. The Emperor's artisans had also been hard at work carving the miniature shield, bow and arrow for the baby to hold. The craftsmanship was quite remarkable down to the last ornate detail. The Emperor would surely be pleased.

This morning, well before sunrise, the Emperor, his wife and all of their relatives and invited friends had gathered in the courtyard, waiting to witness the blessed event. As soon as the day broke, Etta entered the courtyard carrying the naked infant and a full water-jar. When she had reached the front of the crowd, she placed the water-jar on the ground and held the infant for all to see, saying, "You have come into this world by the great kindness of the gods. You will be a valiant, fierce warrior. Your mission in life will be to give the great Sun God the blood of many enemies to drink so that He will be content and will continue to shine down upon us."

After this, she wet her fingers in the water-jar and dropped water on the baby's mouth and chest saying, "Receive this water. It will wash and clean your heart. May it live there forever."

The midwife then lifted the baby up four times to present him to the gods. Next, taking the miniature weapons that the infant clutched in his tiny hand, and lifting them to the sky, she implored the gods, "Use your immeasurable powers to help this boy become a courageous warrior, so that when he leaves this earth he will go into your heavenly palace where those who die bravely rest and rejoice."

Etta then approached the Emperor and his wife and held the baby towards them saying, "These are your beloved parents. You shall respect and obey them for the rest of your days." She paused, then solemnly added, "Your majesties, I present to you your newly named son. With the power you have given me, I have chosen the name Axolo for this child and he shall hereafter be known by this name. May he always be worthy of it."

"Axolo," repeated the king, jubilantly. "A fine, strong name Etta. You have chosen well."

"Thank you, my lord," replied the midwife as she bowed and placed the child in Mia's outstretched arms.

"Let us move to the great hall," shouted Toltec. "Where we shall celebrate the healthy and safe arrival of our new son, Axolo!" The guests cheered and followed Toltec and Mia into the palace.

Kan had just reached the palace doors when Etta grabbed his tunic, preventing him from moving forward without drawing undue attention to himself. Soon, they were alone in the courtyard.

"The Emperor wants to know if everything went according to plan," whispered Etta.

"The baby is with the witches now and is dead to this world," replied Kan for he had no reason to believe otherwise. Etta gave a sigh of relief tinged with sadness, then said, "The Emperor will be pleased." She released his tunic and went to join in the festivities. Kan, however, remained behind. How could he be in the same room with Toltec knowing that he had failed in one of the most important assignments of his life, one that could effectively cause the downfall of the Aztec Empire? He feared that Toltec's piercing black eyes would be able to peer into his soul and discern the truth.

After finding the basket gone, he had been as frenzied as a rabid wolf, searching the entire shore for any trace of the infant. But as the sun began to fall in the sky, the part of his brain still bent on survival screamed at him to escape before the witches arrived, and he had done just that.

Since then, Kan had castigated himself daily for his inexcusable error. But he did not go so far as to tell the Emperor of his mistake. The Emperor believed the last-born son was evil and dead to the mortal world, and that Axolo was now the last son living and, therefore, successor to the throne. Revealing the truth now would only cause the Emperor and his wife unnecessary grief, Kan rationalized. If the baby were miraculously found unharmed, then he would reconsider his options. But the possibility seemed slight.

Kan decided to return home. If asked, he would feign sickness. One more lie to add to his collection, he thought mirthlessly.

CHAPTER SIX

Elsewhere in the Empire, at the edge of the forest, two tiger salamanders circled each other in a silent primeval dance on the bottom of a mossy freshwater pond. The mating ritual had begun. Soon the male salamander caught up with his partner and rubbed his broad head and chin on her yellow-striped back for several minutes. When he finally turned away, she followed him, as if adhering to a carefully written script.

Suddenly, he stopped and deposited a jelly-like substance on a small, flat rock. She then climbed on the rock and sat there as if resting from the earlier game of tag. When she left the rock, the jelly-like packet had disappeared and she seemed to be a little plumper. She slowly moved off into deeper water and her partner walked away in the opposite direction. He would never see her again.

Two days later, she laid her fertilized eggs in the water and carefully attached each one individually to an underwater leaf or twig, hoping that at least some would survive. After fastening the last egg to a long blade of grass, she crawled out of the pond and darted toward a nice, dark hollow log in which she would make her home until the next mating season. Her many as-yet-unborn children would now have to fend for themselves.

Three weeks later, on a beautiful spring morning the eggs began to hatch. The newborn aquatic larvae were about five inches long and had bushy external gills, a dorsal fin and tiny legs.

It would be months before they would begin to resemble their amphibious parents. Their little bodies were a yellowish-green color except for one wide golden stripe down their backs.

Tez was one of the last ones to hatch. Instinctively, he swam out from under the twig to which he had just recently been attached and looked around for underwater insects, for he was a carnivore and a hungry one at that. He was surprised to see hundreds of creatures that looked just like him swimming in the same body of water. Looks like I may need to fight for my food, he thought uncomfortably. Hours later, he stretched out on what seemed to be a large grey rock etched with strange markings and partially covered with algae. He was finally full but exhausted from the effort of catching his first meal.

Suddenly, it felt as if the earth were violently trembling. Tez gripped the 'rock' with his 18 toes, indignant that he might be killed so soon after hatching. At the same instant, he realized the 'rock' he was on was attached to a large, ugly beast with a scaly head, four large wrinkly legs and a long tail made up of a series of large triangular plates. I'm in big trouble here, thought Tez in despair.

Abruptly, the beast began to move and Tez watched in horror as it lunged forward, time and again, with its mouth agape, snapping up the other larvae before they even knew they were in danger. Tez tried desperately to scream to warn the remaining few, but soon realized that salamanders are not able to speak. He then tried to close his eyes to block out the carnage but found he had no eyelids. "Who came up with this ridiculous design?" he wondered, fighting hysteria.

"I did you ungrateful little amphibian," thundered a low voice that apparently was able to hear his unspoken thoughts. The snapping turtle, on which Tez was riding, was startled by the loud roaring voice and dropped down on the muddy pond floor, quickly pulling in its head and legs. The sudden movement caused Tez to slip off the turtle's shell. Tez was trembling and his head whipped back and forth as he searched for a body to put with the voice. "It must belong to something incredibly monstrous since even the snapping beast seems to be afraid of it," thought Tez.

"If I were you, you slimy fish bait," whispered the voice as if it were right behind him, "I would escape before the turtle, or beast as you call it, emerges again from his shell."

With images of the slaughter still replaying in his head, Tez quickly heeded the advice of the disembodied voice. He used his tiny dorsal fin to swim through the pond waters away from the beast and toward a pile of twigs under which he decided he would hide until he thought of a better plan.

"You prodded me to action while I was still in a state of shock. Thank you whoever you are," thought the grateful salamander. "I owe you my life."

"You certainly do," replied the voice pompously. "Because I not only just saved you from certain death, but I created you as well. For I am Tlaloc, the mighty Rain God. Bow down in my presence and praise my name. Remember what I did for you today, you puny scrap of larvae, for I may have use for you in the future. Although for the life of me, I can't imagine why."

"I will wait for your call, my lord," thought Tez, but he was disgusted with himself. How could he ever hope to help the Rain God if he couldn't even obey his first command, which was to bow in his presence. He had tried every contortion he could think of, but bowing was clearly not possible with this body.

"Maybe this Rain God created me as a joke to amuse him in his spare time," Tez grumbled to himself, then yawned. He suddenly realized how tired he was. So much had happened that he felt like he had been alive for years. How could he possibly survive another day? With this question ringing in his tiny brain, he fell into a deep sleep.

****

Miraculously, Tez continued to avoid his predators, even the wily diving beetle, while satisfying his increasing appetite by eating worms, snails and small water insects. Then, one evening, he woke up and felt different. He swam over to a piece of obsidian rock, in which he had seen his reflection many times before, and was amazed at what he saw. His dorsal fin had vanished and so had his external gills. His legs and arms were longer and his coloring had changed. He was now black with yellow spots.

"I'm maturing quite nicely," Tez said to himself, as he strutted back and forth in front of the obsidian mirror. Suddenly, he felt an uncontrollable urge to leave the pond. He scuttled over to the edge of the water and carefully climbed up onto the dry earth. His throat automatically expanded, pushing the outside air into his body for the first time. He quickly turned and darted back into the water and was delighted to find that with this 'new' body he was equally at home in or out of the water.

Eager to explore the world, he emerged from the pond again and was surprised to find that the leaves made a crunching sound under his feet. Understandably fearful of unknown predators, Tez scanned the area for somewhere to hide where he could observe his new surroundings safely. Off to his immediate left, was an old hollow log that appeared deserted. Tez cautiously crept inside. Overhead, a large owl circled, taking advantage of the full moon to search the ground for a delicious midnight snack.

Catching sight of the salamander, Omo the owl silently swooped down but just missed catching the tail as Tez scooted inside the log, oblivious to his fortunate escape.

"If I were ten years younger, that salamander wouldn't have stood a chance," muttered Omo to herself as she perched on top of the hollow log. At that moment, a large dark cloud first obliterated the moon, then slowly transformed itself into the shape of a giant man as it floated down and hovered directly in front of the owl. Omo was not frightened for she had been approached by the Rain God many times before. She knew that she was supposed to receive and obey Tlaloc's orders without question or comment, so she respectfully bowed her head and waited for the great god to speak.

"Hey, what's going on?" Tez thought to himself. He briefly considered leaving the log to investigate, but immediately froze in his tracks when he heard the familiar voice of the Rain God directly overhead.

"My trusted servant, I have an assignment for you. Not far from here in a humble hut, at the base of the volcano, Polpocatepetl, live two sorcerers. A male infant has been placed in their care. His name is Matzin and he has been chosen by the gods to be the next Emperor of the Aztec nation. The sorcerers are of course completely capable of performing their parental duties or they would not have been selected for this important task. But, as you know, a sorcerer's magic is used only for good and is not as effective at night when the forces of evil dominate.

"Therefore, we need a nocturnal creature to protect Matzin during the night and keep him free from harm until he takes his rightful place on the throne, fulfilling his destiny. If you fail, the Empire will be destroyed and the consequences will be dire. Is this clear?"

Both the owl and the salamander nodded their heads. Moments later, the man-shaped cloud dissipated and the moon shone brightly once more. Omo the owl sighed and took off in the direction of the volcano.

Tez cautiously poked his broad head out of the log and

unsuccessfully looked once again for the source of the voice. He was bursting with pride. "He has appointed me, a lowly salamander, to protect the future king of the Empire. This new body of mine must have hidden capabilities that I'm not even aware of." And with that, he exited the log, ready to start his new job. But there was just one small problem. What on earth was a volcano?

CHAPTER SEVEN

Time passed quickly in the forest clearing. Ama and Ollin were constantly kept on their toes because their son seemed to have an insatiable curiosity about everything. He was constantly putting things in his mouth that didn't belong there or climbing into places that weren't meant for small boys. And once he started talking, the questions were unceasing as if he wanted to learn everything about the Empire before he reached the age of 10.

Fortunately for Omo the owl, Matzin expended all his seemingly boundless energy during the day, so by nightfall the owl merely had to stand watch over the entrance to the hut to make sure no unwanted intruders disturbed Matzin's much-needed sleep.

Omo was surprised to find that she felt quite protective toward Matzin, even though she rarely saw him awake. There was something so endearing about the way he held the corner of his blanket in his tiny fist and unconsciously rubbed the material back and forth against his cheek. If he was startled awake from a bad dream, which was rare, Omo would softly hoot in soothing tones, which seemed to immediately comfort the boy and send him back into a deep, peaceful sleep.

One morning, while Omo was slumbering in a nearby tree, Matzin was sitting cross-legged on the floor of the hut reviewing the previous day's lessons with his mother. He was trying hard to concentrate on what Ama was saying, but the bright sun was shining through the doorway as if inviting him to come outside and play. All of a sudden, out of the corner of his eye he saw a black shape hovering in midair. He quickly turned his head and his eyes widened as he realized that it was Ama's large round obsidian mirror that was floating in the middle of the room. The mirror was about two feet in diameter and was framed with loops of cord so that it could be hung on the wall, which is where it usually was. He started to laugh.

"What a wonderful trick, Mother! Oh please teach me some of your spells, please?"

"All in good time, my son," replied Ama smiling. "But this morning I am going to use this mirror to show you how our wondrous world was created. Think of it as history brought to life. Gaze into the mirror, Matzin. What do you see?"

"My reflection, of course," answered Matzin, somewhat disappointed.

"That is because your mind is telling your eyes that, based on past experiences, a reflection is what you are supposed to see when you gaze in a mirror. But Matzin, our eyes may deceive us. Sometimes things are not as they appear to be or as we expect them to be based on every outward indication. Remember this and it will serve you well.

"This time, my son, close your eyes and picture the mirror in your head. Open your heart and mind to unimagined possibilities."

Ama paused for several minutes, pleased to see that Matzin was trying hard to concentrate. Then she sprinkled some powder from her leather pouch over the mirror and whispered, "Now open your eyes and see what is really there, not what you expect to be there."

Matzin slowly opened his eyes and looked in the mirror but this time his face was not looking back at him. Instead, he could see only darkness sprinkled with intermittent twinkling lights. He felt Ama take hold of his hand.

"Shall we investigate further?" Ama asked.

"What do you mean, Mother?" responded Matzin, thoroughly confused. "What I see in the mirror is only an illusion; one of your tricks, isn't it?"

"Who is to say what the truth is? Don't ever let others tell you what to believe. Discover the truth for yourself," Ama replied. Just then, the mirror slowly floated to the ground and lay there face up. Ama gently stepped on to the mirror and motioned for Matzin to do the same. At first he held back. Ama had performed numerous tricks before, but she had never acted so mysterious, and Matzin was somewhat frightened.

"Be strong, Matzin, as befits a true Aztec. Face your fears and conquer them."

Matzin took a deep breath, closed his eyes and stepped onto the mirror, all the while holding tightly to Ama's hand. There was a strange sucking noise and then it felt like a giant serpent had swallowed them whole. Something powerful squeezed him so tightly he could hardly breathe.

"Mother, what's happening?" he screamed as he gasped for air.

"Be brave, Matzin," his mother replied but her voice seemed far away although he still held her hand in a viselike grip.

"I love you Mommy," Matzin whispered as he rubbed her hand on his cheek and then everything went black.

CHAPTER EIGHT

When Matzin finally regained consciousness, he was amazed to find himself floating in a starlit sky with Ama right beside him.

"Where in the world are we, Mother?"

"Well we're not actually in the world as you know it. That world has yet to be formed. We have traveled to the dawn of creation. The place you saw in the mirror."

Matzin was dumbfounded. He knew his mother was one of the most revered sorcerers in the Empire. His father had told him so. But he had no idea that she was able to travel through time. He pulled himself into a sitting position but then wished that he hadn't. His face felt warm and clammy and his stomach was churning.

"I don't feel well," he moaned.

"I'm sorry love. I should have warned you not to make sudden movements so soon after such a trip. Your body is not yet acclimated to this new environment. But then again, I never said learning history would be easy." Ama chuckled.

"Very funny, Mother," Matzin said with a sickly smile.

Within minutes, however, Matzin felt well enough to move around and observe his surroundings.

"Not much to see here, is there?" Matzin said as he looked around at the seemingly endless night sky.

"If we are to see anything worth remembering here we must float up above the stars. But it requires great strength and self-control to propel yourself upward in this atmosphere. Do you feel equal to the task?" asked Ama.

Eager for an adventure, Matzin nodded.

"Have you ever seen a tiger salamander swim underwater?" Ama asked.

"Yes many times."

"Then imagine that you are that salamander and move your arms and legs accordingly."

Matzin's arms began to move in a propeller-like fashion and his legs flipped back and forth. Soon he felt himself rising, at first slowly and then with increasing speed. They navigated their bodies around clusters of stars and narrowly missed being hit by comets or "smoking stars," as Ama called them. Presently, the sky became dark blue in color, then turquoise as they left the stars behind them.

Straight ahead was an immense three-story palace, the walls of which were inlaid with intricate mosaics made of turquoise and jade. The front door was solid gold and four times the height of Matzin's father. Matzin had never seen such opulent beauty. He started to wind his way toward the palace to get a closer look when all of a sudden a bloodcurdling scream made him rush back to Ama's side.

"Come on Mother. It sounds like whoever lives there is in pain. We must do something."

Ama smiled. She was proud of her son for overcoming his obvious fright to help someone in need. Matzin was blissfully unaware that he had just passed an important test of his moral character, she thought to herself.

"You are correct that the inhabitant of that house is in pain but unfortunately there is nothing we can do to alleviate it. The good news is that it will soon be over. Follow me and see for yourself."

Ama floated up to the uppermost window of the palace and

motioned for Matzin to quietly look inside. There, squatting on the floor, in obvious pain, was an imposing creature at least three times as tall as his mother with round dark eyes, a flat, broad nose and a square jaw. On its head was an elaborate headpiece made entirely of bright turquoise-colored feathers. From its ears dangled immense gold circular earrings. Like Matzin, it wore a loincloth but its upper body was also covered by a beautifully embroidered red and black tunic.

The creature's screams suddenly became loud grunting noises and then, to Matzin's amazement, a head popped out between the creature's legs.

"Who is that? What is happening?" whispered Matzin anxiously.

"That is Ometeotl, the most ancient god of the universe. It exists in both a male form and a female form. Right now its female form is in the process of giving birth for the first time."

The creature caught the baby as it fell from her womb and placed it on a nearby mat. Then, she resumed her squatting position and proceeded to push out three more monstrous babies, all boys, oblivious to her uninvited guests peeking in at the window.

"Look Mother," Matzin whispered pointing at the babies. "Each of the boys has a slightly different coloring."

"Very observant of you Matzin," replied Ama delightedly. "They are indeed different hues and are named accordingly. The first son is the Red God, then the Blue God, then the Black God, and finally the White God. These four boys will be responsible for creating the earth as well as all of the other gods. With the birth of these babies, a cycle of creation and destruction begins that continues to our present day." Ama took hold of his hand. "It's time to move on, son. Hold on tightly."

Matzin heard the familiar sucking sound and braced himself for the almost unbearable lung-crunching sensation, but was pleasantly surprised to feel only a slight pressure around his belly this time. When the pressure disappeared he opened his eyes and found himself lying next to Ama in a field surrounded by oak trees with a creek meandering nearby. "What a peaceful place this is," thought Matzin gratefully. The sun shone so brightly above them that Matzin shielded his eyes with his forearm.

"What an adventure that was! But I have to admit it feels good to be back in our own time and our own world."

"Well, actually, this is not our world, Matzin," Ama responded. "In fact, it is not even our sun that shines overhead. It is the very First Sun."

Matzin felt like his head was spinning. He wasn't sure if he even wanted to know what Ama was talking about. He had experienced too many new things today, some of which even challenged what he thought were the immutable laws of nature. His brain felt like a volcano that was on the verge of erupting. He held his head in his hands and shook it back and forth as if that would help the new information settle more easily inside his pounding skull.

"I know you're confused, my love, but it's important that you understand how our world came to be so that you have a healthy respect for the awesome power of the gods. Knowledge is power, Matzin. The more you know, the more you understand and anticipate. Never stop learning new things, my child. I continue to discover new things every day." While she was talking, Ama opened the jaguar-skin pouch hanging around her waist and removed a clay bottle. She pulled out the stopper, poured silver liquid into her palms, and rubbed her hands together. Then, she massaged the liquid into her son's aching forehead. The pain slowly receded and then vanished completely. Matzin sat up and hugged his mother tightly as she kissed his damp, fragrant forehead.

"I don't mean to frighten you further," Ama said. "But we should continue our conversation behind one of these oak trees, so that we are not so visible."

Matzin looked quizically at his mother as they walked toward the nearest tree and settled themselves against its rough, scratchy trunk. Matzin leaned his head against Ama's shoulder and sighed resignedly.

"All right, Mother. Now that my head feels better, I can't stand the suspense! What is the First Sun? And if this is not our world, where in gods' names are we?"

First, Ama quickly scanned the surrounding area, then satisfied that they were safe for the moment, she began to explain.

"As the multi-colored sons of the Duality God matured, they were given the coveted task of creating the world and the creatures that would inhabit it. They were also instructed to create additional gods for the creatures to worship. We now refer to the four sons as the 'creator gods.' The resulting creation, the one you see before you now, was breathtaking and the Duality God was pleased and heartily praised her sons.

Then, the Duality God designated her eldest son, the Black God, as the keeper of the sun. It was his job to move the glowing orb across the sky every day to prevent the dark forces of the night from gaining too much power...."

Just then, the ground underneath them trembled and the air was filled with loud, rhythmic booming noises as if all the drummers in the Empire were pounding on their upright wooden drums. Matzin heard a great ripping sound and something violently thrust him forward, face first into the hard ground. He immediately flipped onto his back and almost fainted. For the tree against which he and Ama had rested only moments ago had been ripped out of the ground by a man, or what appeared to be a man, dressed entirely in black from his feathered headdress to his sandals. He was so monstrous that only the uppermost branches of the torn-out oak tree could be seen in his clenched fist while the tree's roots dangled below.

As Matzin stood there paralyzed with fright, the giant threw his head back and shook the tree up and down over his wide open mouth and chomped down noisily on the acorns that fell inside. Then, still hungry, he turned the tree over and proceeded to chew and swallow all of its thick, sinewy roots. The trunk and branches apparently were not digestible for he flung the remains of the tree into the field narrowly missing Matzin, who at the last second instinctively ducked his head and screamed. The giant looked down.

When he saw Matzin he smiled and reached toward the boy with his enormous arm. Ama, who had been separated from Matzin when the tree was uprooted, raced towards the boy when she saw what was happening. She grabbed his small hand just as the giant envelopped them both in his sweaty fist.

"Don't panic, Matzin," Ama murmured. The giant was holding them so tightly that Matzin was suffocating and the sweat from the giant's palm was stinging his eyes and making him gag. Then, Matzin heard it. The strange sucking sound. Anywhere has to be better than here, he thought, and welcomed the slight pressure on his chest as he and Ama travelled through time yet again.

The next moment he found himself lying in a forest of pine trees that were being moistened by a light rain.

"Well, as I was saying before we were so rudely inter-rupted," Ama said chuckling, once she assured herself that Matzin was all right, "The Black God was in charge of the movement of the sun. But one night, the evil witches of the night transformed themselves into mammoth carnivorous beasts that proceeded to consume every living creature on the earth, destroying every-thing in their path. The next morning, the Black God learned of the complete devastation wrought by the vicious witches and returned to the Duality God's mansion in despair. He prostrated himself in front of its throne and wailed, 'I have failed you most holy one. You and my brothers depended on me to keep our wondrous creation intact. Instead, it lays in ruins, devoured by wicked beasts. Do with me what you will.'

" 'Do not castigate yourself my first-born son,' the Duality God replied. 'This chain of events was fated to happen. There is nothing you could have done to prevent this catastrophe. Don't think for a moment that the witches are more powerful than the most ancient god. I could have counteracted their evil spells had I been so inclined. But there are times when I choose to allow evil to wreak havoc, especially when the end result is consistent with my master plan for the universe. '

" 'Do you mean, this was supposed to happen?' demanded the Black God completely taken aback.

" 'I'm afraid so.'

"Seeing that her son was now thoroughly confused the Duality God said, 'Go get your brothers so that we need only explain this one time.' The Black God left and soon returned with his siblings following close behind. The Duality God motioned for them to sit at the base of her throne.

" 'As you know,' she began, 'the beautiful world that you so painstakingly created has been completely destroyed by the dark forces of the night. And because you worked so hard, we know that you are angry and confused. But what you need to understand is that this annihilation was expected. It was part of our grand master plan for this universe.

" 'Although the four of you are in charge of creating the earth and everything on it, the calendar for that creation was preset by me at the beginning of time and is unalterable. It is called the 'calendar round' and it consists of cycles. Each cycle is made up of 18,980 days or 52 years. For reasons that will forever be beyond your comprehension, and , therefore, will never be revealed to you, the earth will be created by you and then destroyed five times. Each of these creations will be referred to as a Sun.

" 'The First Sun is now over. It is time for you to make another one. Once it is created, neither you nor anyone on earth will ever know exactly when the next Sun will be destroyed. However, there is one rule that is constant. Each Sun can only be destroyed on the last day of a 52-year cycle. But only I know how many cycles will pass before the destruction of that Sun.'

" The four brothers were silent, trying to assimilate this incredible cosmic information. Then, the Black God said, 'My Lord, who will be in charge of keeping the sun in motion during these successive new worlds or "Suns?" I am weary and am not sure if I could perform this task again so soon, unless you wish it of course.'

" 'You are wise to recognize your limitations, my son. Your brother, the White God, shall assume this position for the duration of the Second Sun.' "

Suddenly, Ama stopped speaking and looked overhead. Dark, black clouds had gathered in the already grey sky. What had been a light mist soon became a downpour. Within minutes, Matzin's sandals and loincloth were soaked and water streamed down from his hair into his eyes. Ama once again grabbed his hand.

"We must continue the story elsewhere," she shouted above the din of the storm. Matzin was relieved to hear the familiar sucking sound. He was cold and uncomfortably wet. He hoped their next destination would be as warm and dry as a hearthstone.

Suddenly, without warning, Matzin's wet hand slipped from Ama's grasp. "Mommy!" he screamed but to no avail. The sucking sound had stopped and Ama had vanished.

CHAPTER NINE

Omo the owl was startled out of his daytime sleep by an anxious voice shouting in his ear. She immediately recognized the voice as that of Tlaloc, the Rain God. She swiveled her head toward the noise but Tlaloc had chosen to remain invisible.

"Omo, we have an emergency on our hands. Listen carefully and do exactly as I command."

"Of course, my lord."

"The future king of our Empire has been transported to another Sun and, through an unfortunate string of events, has been separated from his mother, the sorceress, who is at this moment floating between two worlds. The boy is in grave danger, and by the time Ama is able to reverse directions, it may be too late. Therefore, I am sending you to get him to a safe place and wait with him until Ama can return."

"My lord, I am, as always, honored to serve you but with all due respect I am not endowed with the power to transport myself through time...."

"Silence you mangy bird! We're running out of time! Am I not all-powerful? I can transport you to another world with my hands tied behind my back. I would take care of this problem myself but the Duality God strictly prohibits time travel by other gods. Just do as I say. Fly directly into the wind in an easterly direction with your eyes tightly closed. When you feel rain on your wings, open your eyes and you should see the boy below you—hopefully still alive."

Not daring to ask further questions, Omo followed Tlaloc's directions to the letter, even though it was extremely unnerving to fly blind. Suddenly, it felt as if she were going to implode, the pressure was so great on her body. She was incapable of moving her wings. She felt herself going into a free fall and it took every ounce of self-control she had not to open her eyes. Then, just as suddenly, the pressure eased and she felt rain pelting down upon her. She wrenched open her eyes just in time to see the ground below approaching at an alarming rate. She urgently flapped her wings and swooped upward, avoiding a deadly impact by seconds.

Down below, Matzin was nearly paralyzed with fright. He had quickly realized that Ama had unintentionally travelled through time without him. He had no idea when, or if, she would be back. The fierce rain lashing at his almost naked body felt like multiple spears piercing his skin. He shielded his eyes with his hands and searched the surrounding forest for some form of shelter but to no avail.

The water level continued to rise. Soon, he was struggling through rushing water up to his knees. His father had taught him to swim like a fish, but Matzin knew that even an excellent swimmer could drown in raging flood waters. Suddenly, he remembered how his father had soared above the ground when he was in the form of an eagle. Oh, if he only knew the spell of transformation! This information certainly would have been more useful than the other subjects his parents were teaching him, he thought ruefully. What was the use of being the son of two sorcerers if they didn't teach you some of their magic spells?

Then, it struck him. Maybe an incantation wasn't required at all. He recalled imagining that he was a salamander so that he could move through the heavens earlier with Ama. Maybe if he visualized himself as an eagle, he would be able to fly like one.

He scrunched up his eyes and imagined white majestic wings taking the place of his arms and a proud haughty beak replacing his nose and mouth. He flapped his arms up and down and started running through the water hoping to gain the momentum required to soar into the sky.

At that moment, Omo who had been frantically scouring the ground below for the boy, dropped her beak in amazement. What in the gods' names is wrong with the boy? she thought despairingly. Has he gone completely insane flapping around in the flood waters like an idiot instead of trying to reach higher ground? This is supposed to be the future king of the Aztecs? Their savior? Musing on the soundness of this decision, however, was not her job. Quickly, she swooped down, grabbed the boy's loincloth in her powerful claws and used all of her strength to lift Matzin out of the rushing water.

"It worked! I'm flying!" yelled Matzin, startling the owl. And he continued to whoop and holler as Omo climbed upward.

With her strength fading fast under the burden of the boy's weight, and increasingly concerned about the boy's sanity, Omo deposited the boy in the crook of a tree branch, safely above ground. Then, she perched nearby hoping Ama would arrive soon.

Matzin didn't even notice the owl in the branch above him. He was too busy congratulating himself on his flying technique. "Not bad for my first time," he thought to himself and then yawned. Now that he was momentarily out of danger he realized he was exhausted. He leaned against the tree trunk and closed his eyes. All of a sudden, the branch shook wildly and he grabbed it tightly with both hands to avoid falling into the raging waters below. His eyes flew open and there was Ama, miraculously sitting next to him and reaching for his hand. He gripped it with all of his remaining strength and silent tears of relief ran down his cheeks. He was determined to travel with her this time.

"Enough adventures for one day, I think," Ama said. Matzin merely nodded, not trusting himself to speak.

"I'll say," muttered Omo, as she gripped Ama's cloak with her talons.

The familiar sucking noise enveloped the three of them and Matzin was sure he had never heard a sweeter sound. He was so relieved to be with Ama again that he didn't even mind the gut-wrenching pressure around his lungs and stomach. The owl, on the other hand, was gasping for air, unsure of whether she would make it back in one piece.

****

When they returned to their hut, a nice, warm fire was burning in the hearth where a big pot of Ama's delicious azole was simmering on the hearthstones. Matzin reached over and hugged his mother. "I'm so glad to be home....We are home aren't we?"

"Yes, Matzin. This time we're home in our own Sun and for that you should be thankful. I know that I am."

After changing into dry clothes and eating a hearty lunch, Matzin said, "I assume the world we were just in was the Second Sun?"

"No, my love. That was the Fourth Sun. As I told you earlier, the White God presided over the Second Sun. However, that world was soon destroyed by hurricanes at the end of one of the 52-year cycles. For the next world, or Third Sun, the Duality God chose Tlaloc, the Rain God, to guard over the sun even though he wasn't one of the four creator gods. Tlaloc willingly took on the task but was inconsolable when, under his watch, the world was decimated by fiery rain. Chalchi, the Water Goddess, was appointed the sun's keeper during the Fourth Sun. But as you saw first hand, she was unable to prevent the world from being completely destroyed yet again. This time by raging floods."

"So, the next world that was created, or the Fifth Sun, is the one we currently live in?" asked Matzin.

"Exactly."

"Whom did the Duality God choose to preside over our Sun?"

"She gave this task to Huitzipochtli, the mighty Sun God, patron god of the Aztec people."

"But who created the first people to live on this new world?"

"The Duality God sent the White God to the underworld and instructed him to gather up bones from the generations of people that had lived on the previous Suns. The White God then sprinkled these bone fragments with his own life force, or blood, before scattering them all over the earth. The White God's blood miraculously transformed the bones into living women and men. And because the bone fragments were different shapes and sizes, no two humans are exactly alike."

Matzin was silent, digesting this incredible information. Then, all of a sudden, his face registered concern.

"What's troubling you Matzin?" asked Ama.

"I just remembered something that you told me while we were time travelling. You said that the world was going to be created and destroyed five times. Does that mean that our Sun, or world, is the last one?"

Ama nodded.

"Do we know how it will be destroyed?"

Ama looked searchingly at Matzin and asked, "Do you really want to know?"

Matzin sat quietly for a short while, then answered unhesitatingly, "Yes, I want to know. After all that I have learned today, I would like to hear how the story ends."

"Very well. It is said that the Fifth Sun will be detroyed by massive earthquakes and that any survivors will be devoured by flying sky monsters."

Matzin's eyes widened. "Flying sky monsters? Amazing! When will this happen?"

"No one knows, except for the Duality God of course. But, as I told you, the cessation of a Sun, or world, can only occur on the last day of a 52-year cycle."

"When does the next cycle end?" Matzin asked anxiously.

"In 15 years."

"Oh, that's all right then" said Matzin relieved, "I'll be an old man by then."

Ama chuckled. "That's right, my son. You'll have attained the ripe old age of 23."

She was still laughing as Ollin entered the room proudly holding a basket of fresh fish. "Look what I caught today, with very little effort I might add. It was as if the fish were fighting over who would be the first one to leap into my hands. I've never seen anything like it."

"Thank you Ollin. They will taste delicious with my fresh-ly-baked tortillas for lunch tomorrow," Ama said.

"So how did your lessons go this morning, Matzin?"

"Oh Father!" Matzin burst out excitedly, "It was an incredible morning full of adventures! We saw the Duality God giving birth to the four creator gods, a giant almost swallowed us on the First Sun and I almost drowned on the Fourth Sun but I saved myself by becoming an eagle and soaring above the wreckage."

Ollin looked at Ama and raised his eyebrows. She shrugged her shoulders.

"Then," Matzin continued, "Mother explained to me about the 52-year cycles and how our world will eventually be destroyed."

"You're talking faster than a hummingbird flies, my son. It sounds like you've accomplished a lot for one day. Come help me clean up the storage shed and you can give me more details."

"Very well, Father", Matzin replied, as he followed Ollin outside, oblivious to the sleeping owl perched above the door.

CHAPTER TEN

The Empress Mia was sitting on a stone bench in the royal gardens, heedless of the brightly colored flowers, trees and hedges that the servants so painstakingly cared for every day. Her thick black hair, now streaked with grey, was pulled back from her forehead by a turquoise-feathered headband. She lovingly fingered the jade pendant that Toltec had given her when Axolo was born. Where had all the years gone? she wondered. Her only surviving son had just turned 15 and it seemed like only yesterday that she had cradled him in her arms, singing lullabies.

Yet this afternoon he would leave his parents to live at the calmecac school, the school for those of noble birth or those destined to become priests. She had been dreading this day for weeks and she was sure her husband felt the same way, as much as he tried to hide it. She knew Axolo had to receive a formal education and advanced weapons training to be worthy to inherit the Empire and to become a great warrior, but oh how she wished she could postpone the inevitable just a little longer. She sighed, stood up, and walked slowly into the palace.

Emperor Toltec was walking toward Axolo's sleeping quarters when he heard Axolo's voice raised in anger.

"You imbecile! You nearly spilled that hot chocolatl on my newly-embroidered tunics. Leave before you ruin something else."

The servant, hurriedly exiting backward with a full tray of

food, nearly bumped into Toltec as he scurried away. Toltec was enraged as he entered the room.

"How dare you lose your temper in front of the servants! How easy it is to hurt someone who cannot fight back. I'm ashamed of you!"

As Axolo stared up at him defiantly, Toltec paused and turned toward the window. Axolo's petulant outbursts were not uncommon and Toltec blamed himself. He and Mia had always coddled the boy and indulged his every whim. They, of course, hadn't meant to spoil him but he was a gift from the gods and they had treated him accordingly. The calmecac school, with its rigorous discipline, would be a rude but necessary awakening for the boy. Although Toltec would miss him dreadfully, he felt it was none too soon for Axolo to learn self-control, one of the most important characteristics of a true Aztec man.

Toltec turned back towards Axolo and said, "In the calmecac school you will not be pampered. Because you are my son, the teachers will push you harder to make you worthy of the title that you will inherit. They will intentionally humiliate you until you learn to control yourself. Remember that you represent this family while you are there. We expect to hear good reports regarding your progress. Do I make myself clear?"

"I will be the best warrior that school has ever seen, Father," Axolo replied fiercely.

Toltec looked up at his tall, bronzed son, with his broad chest, muscular arms and legs and fire in his eyes. "I don't doubt it my son. But it is equally important to be a good man."

****

Later that afternoon, Axolo was accompanied by his servants to the front of the calmecac school. The school was located at the center of the city inside the high walls that enclosed the main ceremonial district. Within this enclosure, the most dominant structure was, of course, the great temples of the Sun and Rain Gods. The ball court was also found here and Axolo looked forward to exhibiting his prowess as a player.

The calmecac school was inside of a rectangular stone building with a flat roof and about a dozen steps leading up to its entryway. A teacher, who was also a priest, was standing in the opening, greeting the new students who were arriving. Axolo strode up the steps two at a time and pushed his way through the group of young boys until he was standing directly in front of the teacher. The teacher pointedly ignored him and directed the other boys who had arrived first to their sleeping quarters.

Axolo grew impatient. "Do you know who I am?" he demanded, "My father will be displeased to hear how I've been treated so far!"

"On the contrary," replied the teacher in a well-modulated tone, "I think he will be most pleased. The sleeping quarters are to your right at the end of the hall. After you have put away your personal belongings go to the classroom on the other side of the building for further instructions."

Axolo curtly dismissed his servants, then walked inside, purposefully snubbing the teacher. The teacher smiled, knowing that Axolo was in his hands now.

****

Axolo sank wearily onto his bedmat in the large sleeping quarters that housed 20 boys. The morning hours had been devoted to learning the ancient songs and poetry that had been passed down from generation to generation. In addition, the students had practiced public speaking and proper salutations.

After a meager midday meal, which Axolo felt would not even have been fit for his servants to eat, the students were assigned various menial tasks. Axolo was directed to gather firewood from the wooded areas outside of the city, bind the wood together in manageable bundles, and carry the bundles to the school on his back. As the sun sank behind the twin temples on top of the Great Pyramid, the students were given water and tortillas and sent to bed.

Axolo's stomach growled as he lay upon his bedmat. He had never eaten so little nor worked so hard in his life. He, the future Emperor of this nation, was being treated worse than the lowliest servant in his father's palace. It was an outrage! To make it worse, thought Axolo, the teachers seemed to thrive on singling him out for punishment. Well, let them just try to break me, he thought. He came from a long line of great warriors and was determined to bring honor to his family. But to remain strong I need to sleep, he reminded himself, as he closed he eyes and tried to squelch his thirst for not only water, but revenge.

In the middle of the night, Axolo was roughly shaken awake by Teo, one of the harshest teachers at the calmecac. Teo was wearing the standard priestly garb: a black tunic unadorned except for a thin leather strap draped over one shoulder and around his hip. Attached to the strap was an incense pouch made of precious jaguar skin. Teo's long jet-black hair covererd Axolo's face as the priest reached over and pulled Axolo off of his mat.

"What is going on?" demanded Axolo.

Teo slapped the boy across the face. "As you were taught yesterday, but apparently were not bright enough to remember, any questions addressed to your elders and teachers must always include 'tzin' attached to their name, the ultimate sign of respect."

Axolo knew that Teo would like nothing better than for Axolo to argue with him or, better yet, strike back, so he could punish Axolo further. Axolo refused to give Teo that satisfaction.

"You are right, Teotzin. I deeply apologize if I have offended you. May I be so bold, Teotzin, to ask why I was awakened in the middle of the night?"

Teo, taken aback by Axolo's apparent obeisance, was momentarily speechless. Quickly recovering, he responded, "Tonight, and every night hereafter, until you capture your first prisoner in battle, you must exit the city by the southern causeway. Where the causeway meets the mainland you will find a large maguey plant. Detach an agave thorn from the plant and pierce your ears and legs with it, drawing blood each time. Then, immerse yourself in the nearby lake. This will begin the process of hardening your body to both pain and cold and shall be your nightly penance."

Axolo, desperately hoping this was a nightmare from which he would soon awaken, walked out of the calmecac building and into the moonless night towards the towering snow-capped mountains to the south. As he reached the end of the causeway, he briefly entertained the notion of fleeing into the mountains and living off the land, free from all of these oppressive rules and traditions. But then, just as suddenly, he laughed out loud. A harsh laugh, devoid of joy.

"Me, run away? Never! They think a little self-mutilation will make me run from my rightful place on the throne? This bloodletting will merely prepare me for enduring wounds in battle, although I plan on inflicting many more than I receive. No one shall prevent me from being the Emperor, especially not you Teotzin!" And with a strident warrior's cheer he yanked a large thorn off of the maguey plant and plunged it into his thigh.

****

Drenched and shivering, with the holes in his body just beginning to scab over, Axolo reached the calmecac building. Even though the sun had not yet risen, all of the students were awake and busy with their respective chores. Axolo, hungrier than ever after his long journey, approached one of the boys and asked, "Have I missed the morning meal?"

"No," replied the boy who also appeared to be recovering from self-inflicted wounds; "There are no meals today. Only water. It is a day of fasting for further penance we are told."

"Of course it is," mumbled Axolo disgustedly as he approached the priests for further instructions.

****

The sun had just begun to sink behind the western mountains. Brilliant hues of violet, orange and red streaked across the sky as if the gods had set it ablaze. But Axolo was too excited to notice. He was carrying a quiver of obsidian-tipped arrows and had his bow slung over his shoulder as he left the city and walked along the southern causeway towards the mountains.

The calmecac students had endured many months of humiliation at the hands of the priests and Axolo had longed to strike back at them for treating the son of an Emperor in such a fashion. But with great difficulty he held his temper in check. He knew that the priests had the power to expel him, disgrace his family, and prevent him from getting the weapons training he needed. Axolo wanted to become one of the elite corps of warriors, a 'jaguar knight,' which would require many hours of disciplined training and the capture of at least three enemies in battle. Then, he would command the respect he deserved. The same priests who now belittled him would bow in his presence, swearing allegiance to him as their new Emperor.

With that mental picture in his head he laughed exultantly as he switched the bow to his other shoulder and focused on the task ahead. He had been told to go hunting in the mountains. If he brought back enough food to feed the whole school for one whole day, he would be eligible to participate in the tree-climbing contest tomorrow, which was a great honor in and of itself. But, most importantly, as far as Axolo was concerned, whoever won the contest would be chosen to train with the jaguar knights.

Axolo pitied the man who had to face him in his first battle. For by then the anger that continually ate away at his insides, causing nightly stomach pain and headaches, would finally erupt like a volcano in the face of the enemy, in a socially acceptable manner.

Soon, Axolo reached the end of the causeway and walked past the hateful maguey plant. Glancing down at his scab-filled legs, he was thankful that his hunting chore exempted him from the nightly stabbing ritual. As Axolo crept through the forest in search of prey, the sun was swallowed by the mountains and the vibrant celestial painting was erased; leaving in its place a somber, black canvas pinpricked with lights.

CHAPTER ELEVEN

"Becoming invisible does not require a magic spell, my son. It is merely a factor of successfully camouflaging yourself within your immediate surroundings."

"Like a chameleon?" Matzin asked his father wonderingly.

"Exactly. But since we cannot literally change the color of our skin, we must adopt the characteristics of elements in our environment so that we become that element as far as the human eye is concerned."

Ollin paused as he saw Matzin's eyes glazing over in confusion. And who could blame him? Ollin was basically making this up as he went along. Of course, there was a spell of invisibility. It was so basic, in fact, that Ollin had learned it shortly after he learned to walk. But Matzin did not know that he was destined to be an Emperor not a sorcerer and, therefore, believed he had magical powers. Ollin was left with the unenviable task of teaching his son to become invisible without a spell.

"Maybe an example will help," Ollin continued. "If I am in a forest, what is the dominant feature?"

"Trees."

"Correct. In a forest you expect there to be trees. There are so many, in fact that you don't glance at each one individually. Instead, your eye is drawn to things that are different from the trees. An animal's quick movement or an insect rustling among the leaves. Therefore, the more successfully you adopt the characteristics of the dominant feature of your environment, trees in this example, the more invisible you will become."

"I'll try it!" Matzin exclaimed. "Close your eyes and count to twenty. Then see if you can find me. Ready, Father?"

"Ready. But don't wander too far."

Ollin shut his eyes and began counting while Matzin silently crept through the forest. When he came to a particularly thick grove of trees, he examined them carefully. He noticed that the trunks often grew upward at an angle searching for sunlight and the branches were not completely straight but instead were bent as if they had elbows. After staring at them for several seconds, he closed his eyes and visualized himself as a tree. In his mind's eye thick roots pushed through the bottom of his feet and sank into the moist, brown soil. His arms transformed themselves into branches narrowing the further they got from his body, which had become a gnarly old trunk. He remained perfectly still— anchored to the earth at an odd angle by his strong roots. From far away he heard Ollin yell "Twenty!"

Ollin was just about to begin his search when he heard Ama calling for him in an urgent tone. "Matzin will just need to remain 'invisible' a little longer," he thought as he strode quickly toward the hut. As he approached the familiar clearing, he saw Ama standing in front of the food shed with her arms around a young man who was out of breath and visibly distraught.

"Oh Ollin. Thank goodness you heard me. There is no time to waste. This is Colco. His mother has been having periodic seizures, one of which has left her partially paralyzed. The resident sorcerers have been unable to cure or even diagnose her illness. This morning she apparently had a massive stroke and has lapsed into a coma."

"My father always spoke very highly of you both and claimed that it was a true loss for our great city when you moved away," said Colco softly with tears streaming down his brown cheeks. "When my mother lost consciousness, I ran here as quickly as I could, knowing that you were our last hope."

"Who is your father, young man?" asked Ollin.

"His name was Xeta, Ollintzin", replied Colco. "He died the death of a brave warrior in the most recent battle. I am his eldest son and the man of the house now."

Ollin walked towards Colco and embraced him. "I knew Xeta well. He was a fine man. By his labors he has won a noble death and he now rightfully resides in Our Lord's palace of delights. You should be proud."

"I am, but I miss him terribly. Thank you, Ollintzin."

Ama quickly brought them back to the matter at hand. "Ollin, I feel it would be best if you go alone. Colco's mother needs immediate care and if you become an eagle you can reach her well before sundown. I've already filled your pouch with maize, peyotl, extracts of various plants and stones. You can carry it around your neck as you fly."

"You have thought of everything, as always, Ama. Just one of the many reasons that I love you. I will go at once," replied Ollin, kissing her on the cheek.

Within minutes, Colco was running back towards the city . Overhead, a majestic eagle, with a leather pouch around its neck, led the way, momentarily forgetting that in the forest below a young boy was still pretending to be a tree.

Ama watched her husband soar beneath the wispy clouds as the sun sank below the trees. She suddenly realized that with all of the earlier commotion, Ollin had neglected to tell her what he and Matzin had accomplished today. In fact, where was the boy? Matzin knew better than to stay out after dark. He had been repeatedly warned about the witches. Ama walked to the edge of the clearing calling his name but received no response. Her initial reaction was to search for him, but then her good sense took over. He could be anywhere in the forest and could easily return while she was gone. Then, he would worry. The best course of action would be to stay here until Ollin came home. Hopefully, by then, Matzin would have returned unharmed.

CHAPTER TWELVE

Omo stretched out her wings and slowly opened her eyes. It was a beautiful, moonless, starry night. She was quite hungry and looked forward to swooping down on some unfortunate rodents. However, first she flew off of her perch to peek inside the hut and make sure all was well within, as she did every night. Immediately, she knew something was amiss. It was well past dinnertime and yet neither Ollin nor Matzin were anywhere in sight. In fact, Ama, instead of preparing a meal, was kneeling in front of the altar to the gods, earnestly praying.

"What in the gods' name is going on?" wondered Omo, fearing the worst.

"Omo," whispered a familiar voice. Omo's head swiveled around, but there was nothing there. Apparently, the Rain God had decided to remain invisible.

"At your service, my lord" replied Omo, bowing her head, knowing that her question would now be answered.

"Matzin is again in danger. He is in the forest under the misguided belief that he has made himself invisible by becoming a tree. Ollin was supposed to find him but, unbeknownst to Matzin, Ollin has gone to the city to help a sick friend. I need not remind you of the horrifying things that can happen to a human after dark. It is imperative that you find him immediately and somehow bring him home unscathed."

"I will do my best to make you proud, my lord," responded

Omo as she quickly flew toward the forest. "How can this crazy boy be the savior of the Aztec nation?" Omo wondered as she scanned the earth below. "First he thinks he's a bird, and now a tree? What next?" She was getting too old for this job.

* * * * * * * * * * * * * * * * * * * *

Tez, the tiger salamander, was oblivious to all of the commotion surrounding him as he slowly made his way through the forest searching for Matzin, the future king, who needed his humble protection. It had taken a long time for him to reach his destination, fifteen years in fact, and in that time he had grown to his full adult length of 13 inches. The journey had not been an easy one. He had quickly learned that most animals consider salamanders a delicacy. He had spent many days hiding in hollow logs and abandoned burrows. Thankfully, he was equally at home on land or in water, a trait that had saved his life numerous times. Finally, he had reached the forest at the base of the volcano. It shouldn't be long now until he saw the hut that the Rain God had described.

Suddenly, he was completely still, sensing immediate danger nearby. While scanning the area for potential predators, he quickly scooted tail first into a nearby rotten log. Hesitantly peering out of the opening, he saw a strange sight. A human boy-child, dressed only in a loincloth, was standing perfectly still with each of his arms bent in an unnatural position. The only thing moving was the boy's mouth– for he was muttering to himself. Must be some kind of strange Aztec ritual, thought Tez.

"Why hasn't Ollin found me yet?" Matzin murmured. His arms and legs were stiff, sore and tingly from remaining motionless for so long. Not to mention the fact that it was well past his dinnertime and he was starving. He truly did not know what to do. On the one hand he was anxious for Ollin to pass through this part of the forest to see if, in fact, Matzin had succeeded in making himself invisible. On the other hand, the sun had long since set, and Ama had warned him of the evil witches that came out at night and against whom a sorcerer's magic was, for the most part, ineffective. He had been taught that the Aztecs put a high value on obeying one's elders but he was in a quandary. Should he obey Ollin, who asked him to wait until he was found, or Ama who had asked him not to stay out after dark.

"Oh gods, what should I do?" He finally decided that Ollin would never have asked him to stay out here if he had had any idea that the game would last past sunset. So, Matzin was just about to become "visible" again and return home when he heard the crackle of leaves in the distance and someone whistling.

"What a perfect opportunity to see if I've successfully become a tree!" Matzin thought excitedly. He remained completely still, although the pain was excruciating.

****

Axolo was whistling a tune he had recently learned from his music teacher as he walked through the forest on his way to the causeway. His cotton bag, which the priests had given him this morning, was filled with dead animals. He was certain that he had enough meat to feed the entire calmecac for a day and he looked forward to participating in the tree-climbing ceremony tomorrow.

Then, out of the corner of his eye he saw what looked like a giant deer standing completely still. If he came home with a buck, in addition to his full bag, he would be the envy of his classmates. Moving slowly behind a tree so as not to startle the deer, Axolo placed his foot on a rotten log, reached behind him, pulled out one of his last arrows and quietly placed it in his bow.

Tez was startled by a loud thump overhead. What could

possibly have landed on his log? He scooted up the inside wall of the log and looked up through a tiny hole at the top. He was amazed to see a boy's bare human foot. This boy, however, was not posing like a tree. Instead, he was getting ready to use one of those killing implements that he had heard humans call a "bowenairoh." And if Tez wasn't mistaken, this child was aiming his weapon at the other boy posed like a statue.

Omo meanwhile was darting among the trees frantically searching for the future Emperor. Then she saw Matzin and was about to laugh at the spectacle he made when she realized that he was not alone. Poised behind a tree, just out of Matzin's sight, was danger in the form of a boy with an arrow aimed at Matzin's heart. She would never get there in time.

"Matzin, Matzin!" she screeched circling, "Watch out! Drop to the ground! Matzin, Matzin!" She knew it was a futile gesture. Only animals could understand other animals. Matzin would hear only a screeching owl. She dove towards the boy, unconcerned for her own safety. Owls were considered a sacred bird and bad luck befell anyone who killed one.

"Matzin?" Tez exclaimed. "The boy performing what seems like a strange Aztec ritual is Matzin? The boy I have been ordered to protect? Oh my gods!" Tez scooted through the hole in the top of the log and quickly climbed up the hunter's leg and into his loincloth just as Axolo pulled back the bow. Startled, Axolo instinctively reached into his loincloth to remove the intruder and in so doing unintentionally raised the bow and released the arrow.

Omo felt a searing pain as the arrow pierced the tip of her left wing. She desperately tried to stay aloft but it was no use.

"Forgive me Rain God. I have failed you," she murmured just before she struck the ground.

Axolo finally grasped the salamander and flung it away in disgust. If he were going to become a jaguar knight he would have to work on remaining focused on his prey despite any discomfort. He was amazed to see that the deer had not been startled by all the commotion. The gods have given me a second chance he thought as he pulled the last arrow from his quiver. Then, his arm froze in mid-air when he saw what his previous arrow had struck.

He raced to the fallen owl and knelt beside it in disbelief. How could this have happened to him, the chosen one? Then he noticed that the owl's chest was still expanding and contracting, albeit slowly. Perhaps there was still hope. He tore a piece from his cloth bag and wrapped it carefully around the injured wing, hoping to staunch the flow of blood. He then cradled the unconscious bird in his arms and started the long walk back to the city, beseeching the gods to save this sacred owl so that his reign would not be plagued with misfortune. The large deer was forgotten.

****

"I did it! I did it!" shouted Matzin and Tez simultaneously. Tez had landed on the top of Matzin's head after being flung in the air by Axolo. Matzin was so painfully numb from remaining motionless for so long that he didn't even notice.

"I passed my first test," thought Tez exultantly as Matzin whooped with delight.

"That boy knelt right in front of me and saw only the owl! That screeching bird almost caused me to lose my balance. But I didn't! Ollin will be so pleased that I succeeded at becoming invisible on my first try!"

Matzin began to slowly hobble back to the hut, blissfully unaware that he had a hitchhiker on his head.

CHAPTER THIRTEEN

With no moon overhead, it was as dark as the inside of a witches' cave as Ollin walked along the causeway away from the city. He had been unable to fly home because Colco had showered him with gifts, among which were a beautifully embroidered cotton cloak, an intricately designed water jug, and one pound of cacao beans.

Colco's mother had not responded to his initial treatments but, thanks be to the gods, his final concoction of peyotl, ground snail shells, snake bones and a turkey egg had caused her to regain consciousness. Colco was still weeping with joy when Ollin left their home. While ministering to Colco's mother, Ollin remembered that he had left Matzin wandering alone in the woods. The sorcerer hoped that to avoid punishment his son would return home before his curfew at nightfall.

He couldn't wait to get home. He was hungry and tired and this causeway had never seemed longer. "I'm getting old," he thought. Just then he noticed a young man kneeling on the edge of the causeway about four tree lengths ahead of him. He held something in his arms. As he came closer, Ollin saw a fine-looking boy and a bag full of fresh kill on the ground. In a low anguished voice, the boy moaned, "O lord of all creation, O almighty gods in whose hand lies the power of life and death over mortals, what can I do? Have I endured all of this pain and humiliation at the hands of the priests for nothing? Will the only thing I desire be taken from me because of one misplaced arrow?"

Ollin gently placed his hand on the boy's shoulder and asked, "What is troubling you, young man? Perhaps I can be of some assistance."

Axolo had not expected anyone to be traveling along this causeway after nightfall, and was embarrassed that this commoner had seen him lose control of his emotions. If his father heard of this, he would be ashamed. He quickly wiped the tears from his face, then slowly rose and turned towards the stranger, trying to salvage what was left of his dignity.

When Ollin saw the wounded owl in the boy's arms he gasped. No wonder the boy was upset. If the owl died at the hands of this boy a cloud of misfortune would follow him for the rest of his days. Ollin placed his finger on the owl's neck and felt a faint pulse. There was no time to lose.

"Quickly, follow me," commanded Ollin as he strode quickly towards the forest. Axolo's first reaction was anger. How dare he order me about! Doesn't he know who I am? But then he saw the distinctive jaguar-skin pouch hanging from the man's neck.

"You are a sorcerer!" Axolo exclaimed in disbelief.

"Yes," Ollin replied, "But even I won't be able to heal the bird unless we hurry."

Axolo needed no further prodding. He quickly followed Ollin toward the end of the causeway being careful not to jostle the owl. But he came to an abrupt halt when he saw the sorcerer walk straight towards the insidious, large maguey plant. He watched Ollin pull an obsidian knife from his pouch and cut away one of the large pods hidden among the thick leaves, carefully avoiding the long, brutal thorns. The sorcerer used the knife to puncture a small hole in the top of the pod. Placing his mouth over the hole he sucked out the juice or 'pulque' from the pod and immediately spit it into the water jug Colco had given him. He repeated this several times, being careful not to let the pulque linger in his mouth, for even small quantities of the juice could cause hallucinations. Finally satisfied with the amount extracted, Ollin removed a clay vial filled with a bluish-green powder from his pouch and added a pinch of the powder to the liquid in the jug.

"Bring the owl over here," Ollin commanded. The sorcerer was surprised that the boy seemed reluctant to approach him even though he held the potion that could heal the wounded owl, but then he saw the boy's scab-filled arms and legs and understood. Thanks be to the gods that Matzin has been spared the calmecac's form of discipline, he thought. Ollin believed in raising respectful, obedient children, but felt strongly that forcing a child to hurt himself to develop self-control was not the best way to accomplish this goal. He met the boy halfway and gently pried open the owl's beak. Over and over again he reached into the jug and rubbed his wet fingers on the owl's tongue. "Stroke the owl's neck to encourage him to swallow," he instructed the boy. Axolo did as he was told, praying that they were not too late.

When the owl had swallowed the entire potion, the sorcerer placed his hands on its head and recited an incantation in a language Axolo could not understand. The owl's eyes fluttered open and then closed again. Ollin placed his fingers on the bird's throat and was relieved to feel a stronger pulse. "Take him to your home and keep him warm and hydrated. You should see a vast improvement by sunset tomorrow," Ollin instructed.

"You have saved my life, sir. Nothing I can give you could possibly repay you for the gift you have given me, but name your price and I shall see that you are paid," Axolo murmured gratefully.

"Young man, I've been blessed with a fine wife, a wonderful child, a job I enjoy and good health; therefore, I want for nothing. All I ask is that the next time you see a fellow Aztec in need, you will help him as I have helped you. And remember what you have witnessed tonight. I know that you have associated the maguey plant with pain and suffering. But you have just seen how the maguey plant can relieve pain and suffering as well. Everything can be used for either good or evil purposes. Choose wisely."

Ollin reached down to pick up the gifts from Colco that he had placed next to the maguey plant while he was tending to the owl. "Well, it is late and I am weary. We must each be on our way. May the gods be with you."

"And with you, sir," Axolo replied as he watched the sorcerer walk towards the volcanic snow-topped mountains.

****

Omo the owl awoke with a start and was surprised to find herself in a small room, on the floor. Lying next to her on a mat was a muscular young man who looked vaguely familiar. Where was she? Omo wondered, praying that she was not in danger because escape was out of the question. Her wings were completely immobilized by a cloak that was wrapped around her body. She was frustrated because she could recall only her name and that she had an important job to do. But what? She rotated her head towards the sound of approaching feet, and immediately wished she hadn't. The pain was excruciating. Teo, the calmecac priest, walked in the room, and kicked Axolo awake with his foot. "Time to prepare for the tree-climbing ceremony, 'future Emperor,' " he said irreverently, then left.

"That's it!" screeched Omo. "Future Emperor. I've been chosen to guard over the future Emperor to the Aztec throne and keep him free from harm from sunset to sunrise." The owl sighed with relief as she turned her head towards the young man who was now sitting and staring at her. "How fortunate that the priest called him by name or I would not have recognized him. I must have been hit pretty hard to have lost so much of my memory. What could have possibly happened? Well, at least my charge is all right. That's all that matters."

Axolo was beside himself. The sorcerer's potion had worked. The owl was awake and screeching. He immediately gave her a small rodent that he had killed last night for her. Then he loosened the cloak from around her body. Omo bowed her head towards Axolo and devoured her morning meal.

Now that he was no longer worried about the owl's health, Axolo was embarrassed that the sorcerer had seen him so distraught. Had not the gods ordained that he, the last-born son, would be the next Emperor? Had he not been born under the most auspicious sign? Would the gods have let a mere owl stand in the way of his chosen path? Of course not. "The sorcerer was merely placed in my path so that my destiny would be fulfilled," he said to himself. He vowed that never again would anyone see him lose control over his emotions. A lack of self-control was a sign of weakness that could be exploited by an enemy. "I must be more careful in the future," he vowed as he adjusted his loincloth.

Axolo saw that the owl had fallen asleep but this time her breathing was not labored. He would check on her again when he returned victoriously from the tree-climbing ceremony.

****

Twenty days ago, the jaguar and Eagle Knights had cut down one of the tallest trees in the forest and dragged it back to the city into the main temple area. There, the elite warriors hauled it upright and anchored it to the ground. Exiting the calmecac building, Axolo was amazed that although the sun had not yet risen above the Great Pyramid, the temple grounds were already filled with people eager to share in the day's festivities. Low tables, laden with food and drink, had been placed at regular intervals around the perimeter of the plaza, and garlands of red, blue and yellow flowers were strewn all over the ground.

On a platform just below the Great Pyramid, Axolo's parents, Emperor Toltec and Empress Mia, sat behind a table draped with a white cotton cloth. Four beautiful, young women dressed all in white served the royal couple their favorite dishes, such as pheasant and crow, together with freshly made tortillas which the royal couple used to scoop the food into their mouths. The Emperor wore his gold ear plugs and an elaborate jade lip plug in the form of a fire serpent in honor of the occasion and both Toltec and Mia's arms were adorned with multiple bracelets made out of amethyst, turquoise and gold.

Axolo tried to catch his parents' eyes but the crowd was too thick; they could not see him. "No matter," he said to himself, "They'll notice me soon enough, when I am the first to reach the top of the tree." A hush came over the crowd when a man, wearing a white cloak trimmed in red and a necklace of fresh yellow flowers around his neck, blew into a conch shell to start the ceremony.

The crowd parted and murmured respectfully as the elite jaguar knights marched through the precinct gate and toward the tree. They were resplendent in their jaguar-skinned cloaks and fine bone lip plugs. Axolo longed to be so admired. When the warriors reached the base of the tree, they removed the supports, which were holding it upright and began to lower it to the ground, taking care not to injure anyone in the process. Then, the knights walked to the base of the platform upon which the Emperor and his wife were seated and bowed. The four women who had been serving the royal couple picked up baskets filled with sacred paper and thick ropes made from the fibers of maguey plants and handed them down to the warriors. Half of the soldiers methodically wrapped the paper around the tree until it was completely covered, while the others tightly attached the ropes to the top of the tree.

When their tasks were finished, the commander of the jaguar knights again approached the platform. Emperor Toltec was waiting for him with the Xocotl, a little figure made out of dough. The commander took the Xocotl, and attached it securely to the very top of the tree. Then, the warriors lifted the tree until it was completely upright where it was again anchored to the ground.

Emperor Toltec raised his arms and shouted, "Let the feasting begin!" The citizens cheered and surged towards the food tables. Axolo, however, was too excited to eat. Instead he squatted in a corner of the plaza and stared at the tall tree trying to map out the fastest way to climb it. He intended to memorize every hollow and burl before the tree-climbing event began at sundown.

CHAPTER FOURTEEN

Tez, the salamander, was thoroughly enjoying himself even though Matzin kept him on his toes, all 18 of them. A narrow creek, which probably originated high in the surrounding mountains, traversed the forest and ran behind the sorcerers' hut. So, Tez could track Matzin either by land or in the water. Tez preferred the latter since he swam faster than he crawled, but occasionally he would find himself sprinting from hollow log to hollow log trying to keep an eye on his active charge while dodging predators, such as eagles and snakes. But he never missed a meal. There were plenty of insects, worms and snails available in the forest and he slept peacefully in a hole he had made for himself near the opening of the hut.

He was resting in his hole at this moment while Matzin, Ama and Ollin enjoyed their midday meal. "If I am not mistaken, the tree climbing ceremony will take place tonight. I always enjoyed watching that event when we lived in the city. Didn't you Ama?" Ollin asked his wife.

"As I recall you enjoyed the free food and drink as well," Ama replied with a smile.

"Excuse me Father, but what is a tree climbing ceremony?" Matzin asked politely. Ama was pleased. Matzin's manners had greatly improved. He no longer interrupted his parents in the middle of a sentence or talked with his mouth full. This was due in large part to the good examples set by Ama and Ollin.

But, Ama mused, strangely enough, teaching Matzin how to become "invisible" had also strengthened his character. It had taught him the virtue of patience. And, as a result of remaining motionless for hours with nothing else to do but observe his surroundings, he had become very aware of his environment, and noticed the slightest changes within it. Fortunately, Matzin was still a healthy, rambunctious boy, full of energy, Gods be praised, but now he could focus his energy on a task until it was completed or on a problem until it was solved. Both important qualities for a future king.

As Ollin finished describing the tree climbing ceremony and its purpose, Matzin's eyes shone. "Oh Father, it sounds wonderfully exciting! How I wish I could participate."

"Only those who attend the calmecac school to become warriors are eligible to climb, my son. Your destiny lies down a different path."

"I know, I know. A sorcerer. Please don't take this the wrong way, Father. But sometimes I feel that I would be a much better warrior than a sorcerer. I've mastered the spells of flight, invisibility and transformation," Matzin declared, as Ama and Ollin dared not catch each other's eye for fear of laughing out loud, "but so far I've been hopeless at any other incantation. However, each day I feel stronger and faster. I bet I would be a match for any of those calmecac students if I just had some weapons training."

His parents looked at each other, knowing that they were thinking the same thing. Weapons training! While they had been busy making sure that their son embraced the basic virtues of a good king, sound moral judgment, good manners and self-control, all of which were of course essential, they had neglected to prepare him to lead the Aztec people into battle. The Gods would not be pleased.

"You bring up an interesting point, Matzin," Ollin replied

to Matzin's surprise. "Although you are not destined to become a warrior, you should still learn the basics of fighting with weapons. The next time I am in the city I will get a sword for you to practice with. You are already fairly proficient with a spear and bow since you use them for hunting. But there is always room for improvement."

Matzin couldn't believe his good fortune. He threw his arms around Ollin. "Thank you, Father! May I go with you to the city?" His parents had described the city to him in detail and he longed to see it for himself.

"Not this time, my son."

Matzin was too excited about practicing with a real warrior's weapon to be too disappointed about not accompanying his father. "May I be excused, Mother?"

"Yes Matzin. But I would like to have fish for dinner. So, could you please take your spear and practice your technique near the stream?"

Delighted, Matzin grabbed his obsidian-tipped spear, which his father had made for him when he turned 13, and ran outside. He glanced over his shoulder to see if the yellow-specked salamander would emerge from his hole and follow him again. Sure enough, there he was trying desperately to keep up. Matzin slowed his pace to accommodate the amphibian. Matzin was amused that the little creature seemed to want to be with him and he had no idea why. Generally, salamanders avoided humans because salamander meat was considered a delicacy by the Aztecs. Fortunately for this salamander, thought Matzin, I only needed to try that dish once to know it was disgusting. Matzin enjoyed thinking of the salamander as his companion since he had no friends to speak of. He glanced back once again to make sure it was still there and then he headed toward the stream.

CHAPTER FIFTEEN

The setting sun cast an array of colors across the sky as the student warriors waited for the contest to begin. The corps of elite jaguar knights surrounded the raised tree to guard against anyone getting a head start. Suddenly, the sun sank below the temple walls and one of the guards blew through a conch shell to signify the start of the race. Axolo sprinted through the ring of warriors, grabbed a hanging rope and started to climb.

Omo, startled by the haunting sound of the shell, woke from a deep sleep. She was surprised that it was already dark outside and pleased that her wing felt completely healed. She glanced over to check on the boy and was horrified to see that the mat was bare. She flew out of the room and down an empty corridor frantically searching for a way out. Loud cheering and the pounding of drums echoed off the walls as she finally located an opening into the main temple precinct grounds. Omo was amazed to see young men, clad only in loincloths, pulling themselves up a large tree, propped up in the middle of the square. The plaza was filled with Aztec men and women watching the spectacle and cheering.

Omo quickly realized that Axolo was one of the crazy climbers. "Oh why couldn't he be satisfied with being a spectator?" Omo moaned to herself. "How can I possibly save him if he falls?"

Axolo and another student were nearing the top of the tree.

The sweat stung Axolo's eyes, but he dared not let go of the rope, even with one hand to wipe them. Colco, the other student, was gaining on him. It was imperative that Axolo win this contest. A strong ruler was feared; nothing else mattered. And a feared ruler would not be questioned if he avenged himself against certain members of the religious community, namely Teo, Axolo thought with pleasure. He would never forgive the priest for humiliating him, and he would make sure that he paid dearly for it. He also yearned to see the looks of pride on his parents' faces when he emerged victorious.

Axolo was jolted from his reverie when he saw that he and Colco were now head to head. He had not seen Colco for a couple of moons because Colco had temporarily left school to care for his mother who had nearly died. Axolo knew that Colco adored his mother and that she was his sole surviving parent. This gave him an idea.

"Colco!" he cried out. "I was sorry to hear about your mother."

Colco glanced at Axolo with surprise. It was unheard of to have a conversation during this contest.

"Thank you," he replied breathlessly. "Praise be to the gods and thanks to a fine sorcerer, she is feeling much better."

Axolo feigned shock. "Oh, then the rumor isn't true?"

"What rumor?"

'I thought I heard just this morning that your mother had lost consciousness again..."

"What?!"

"I'm amazed this contest is more important to you than being by your mother's side."

Colco's face registered shock and amazement. He felt as if his limbs had turned to stone. Axolo took full advantage of Colco's paralyzed state to pull ahead. He felt a slight twinge of remorse for lying to a fellow student but the stakes were too high to lose and the Xocatl was now within arm's reach. He tried to dislodge the little dough figure from the top of the tree but it seemed to be caught on something. He glanced down, saw other climbers gaining on him, and tugged furiously at the Xocatl but to no avail.

Omo saw that Axolo was distressed. Apparently, it was important for the boy to remove the pasty figure to protect himself from the other young men who were trying to reach him. Without hesitating, Omo swooped down towards the top of the tree, dug her talons into the dough figure and yanked it off. Then, she gently deposited it into Axolo's outstretched hand.

"The gods are surely smiling down upon me to have sent my owl to help me," Axolo thought exultantly, "Clearly they are not displeased with the lie I used to help me reach the Xocatl first."

Axolo lifted the Xocatl high above his head and dashed it against the tree trunk. The ecstatic cheering of the crowd surrounded him like a warm blanket as the pieces of dough fell to the ground.

When the climbers all safely reached the ground, the tree was lowered with a crash. Axolo smirked as he saw Colco sprint toward the temple gates. The chief of the jaguar knights draped Axolo in a brown mantle with an elaborately feathered edge signifying that he was the captor of the Xocatl and, therefore, worthy to be trained as a jaguar knight. Gifts were laid at his feet. He would also be entitled from now on to private sleeping quarters in the calmecac building. His father, unaware of the means by which his son had won the prize, praised Axolo for his strength and endurance and declared that he had all the makings of a fine warrior. Then, Axolo, followed by the priests blowing conch shells and the boisterous crowd, led a procession around the precinct.

Omo, circling overhead, was proud of her charge. He will make a regal Emperor, she thought. But it would be fine with me if he sticks with quieter games like patolli, the dice game, from now on.

****

Axolo, drenched in sweat, opened his eyes and sat up quickly, completely disoriented. He was on his mat in his new room at the calmecac and the owl was watching him with what seemed like concern.

"The nightmare again!" Axolo exclaimed. But he had had it so often that he began to wonder if it was only a recurring bad dream or some kind of omen. He jumped up, wrapped the coveted brown mantle tightly around his shoulders as if it had the power to protect him from harm and went in search of Kan, the high priest. It didn't take long to find him. Kan was in front of the communal hearth warming up some chocatl to drink before he left to perform his temple duties. Upon seeing Axolo, he smiled and said, "Congratulations on your victory last night. You have shown yourself worthy of your destiny." To Kan's astonishment, Axolo waved his hand dismissively, barely acknowledging the praise, and demanded, "Kan, as the high priest of our Empire, you alone are authorized to read and interpret the Tonalamatl, or Book of Destinies, are you not?"

"Yes, of course."

"Then, upon my birth, it was you who determined, with the aid of the tonalamatl, that I would be the successor to the throne?"

"That is correct. Why do you ask?" Kan replied nervously.

"I've been bothered recently by a recurring nightmare that I thought might have some greater significance. But I'm probably mistaken," Axolo added hopefully.

"What kind of nightmare?" Kan asked as he placed his mug on the floor and clasped his hands behind his back so Axolo could not see them trembling.

"Well, in each one, I am in the throne room and my father is walking towards me with a large smile on his face. As he gets closer, he removes the crown from his head and I am filled with indescribable joy because I know that it will soon belong to me. When he is only steps away, I get down on one knee and bow my head in anticipation of the weight. But to my consternation, he walks right past me. I turn my head just in time to see him placing the crown, my crown, on another bowed head. Then my father disappears.

"Enraged, I rush at this impostor to claim what is rightfully mine. The fraud raises his arms to defend himself, revealing what looks like a purple stain on his right upper arm, the shape of which looks disconcertingly familiar to me. Then, as I try to reach for the crown everything turns black and I awaken."

Axolo is shocked to see that Kan is visibly shaken by this story. Without allowing the priest time to regain his composure Axolo cries out, "You are hiding something from me. What is it?"

Kan shook his head, fearful his voice would betray him. Axolo nonchalantly picked up a machete lying near a mound of cacao pods, in the corner of the room, placed a pod on a table, lifted the machete over his head and neatly split the pod in equal halves. "My father abhors liars and subjects them to an especially horrific torture. You must know that." Axolo said as he placed another pod on the table and expertly sliced it in two. Kan, visibly pale and trembling, knew that Axolo was fully capable of fabricating stories to turn the Emperor against him. He had seen him lie many times before if it was to his advantage but had been too fearful to reveal this unsettling character trait to the Emperor. However, he also knew that the Emperor would banish him immediately if he told Axolo the truth, or what Toltec believed to be the truth. There was only one thing to do.

"Axolo, come with me to the palace. This is something that needs to be discussed with your father."

Increasingly concerned, Axolo put down the machete and followed the high priest out of the calmecac building. When they entered the throne room, the warrior captains were just leaving. Upon seeing Axolo, the captain of the jaguar knights clapped him on the shoulder and said, "An incredible performance last night Axolo. We were just planning our next battle, one in which you have earned the right to participate. You will conduct yourself heroically and capture many enemies, of that I am certain."

"Thank you, sir," Axolo replied respectfully, but his mind was on what Kan and his father were going to say. Based on Kan's demeanor, the news was not going to be good.

"Oh gods in the heavens," Axolo vowed silently to himself, "I vow here and now that the humiliation and pain I have endured and continue to endure shall not have been in vain. Regardless of what I hear today, nothing shall deter me from my quest for the crown. Did You not send the owl as my talisman? My father and Kan are, after all, merely humans. They cannot change the destiny You have decreed for me and I will accept nothing less." And with these words reverberating in his mind he approached the throne.

****

Hours later, Axolo's mind was reeling. A twin brother, born under an evil sign, who was considered dead for all intents and purposes, but who actually lived with witches? And his mother knew nothing about it? Remarkable. But Kan and his father had assured him that this story was of no consequence to him. He was still heir to the throne and that was the only thing that mattered. There was, of course, always the possibility that at some point in time the witches would convince this unfortunate twin to try and take over the throne. But, according to Kan, the gods had made the evil twin easy to recognize by placing a purple birthmark on his arm, just like the one Axolo had seen in his dream. Therefore, if his wicked brother even attempted to enter the city, Axolo would make sure that he did not leave it alive.

Chapter Sixteen

Matzin kneeled down next to the icy-cold mountain stream and splashed water on his perspiring face. The sun was already directly overhead in a cloudless sky and he had yet to catch anything for his family's evening meal although he had traveled farther than ever before into the forest. Two days ago he had been very successful with his spear and had caught enough fish for two meals. He knew his parents had been pleased. But today he would be lucky if he returned with a small rodent. He glanced at the little salamander, who was lying completely still on a rock. Since the animal had no eyelids, it was impossible to tell if he was awake or not. His pulsating gills, however, reassured Matzin that the small creature was still alive. My friend must be exhausted, thought Matzin, even though he had traveled along the banks of the stream so that Tez could keep up with him. Matzin realized early on that despite Tez's amphibious nature, the salamander moved more quickly in the water than on land.

Matzin leaned back against a tree and pulled his midday snack out of the leather pouch hanging around his waist. Two tortillas filled with beans. His favorite. Matzin noticed that Tez had slithered back into the water and was stalking underwater insects for his meal. After Matzin finished his last bite, the warm sun, combined with a full stomach, made him feel drowsy. His thoughts turned towards the conversation he had had with his parents that morning. His father was going to the city today to check on Colco's mother. She no longer had fainting spells, but her left arm was still slightly paralyzed. Ollin had concocted a potion that he hoped might help.

Matzin longed to visit the city. When he was a very young boy, he and Ama had accompanied Ollin to the causeway that led to the city, and far off Matzin had glimpsed the magnificent twin temples. Ever since that day, Tenochtitlan had fascinated him and he had begged for stories about this great city that the Emperor called home. Each time Ama or Ollin traveled to Tenochtitlan on business he asked to go too, but they always found an excuse to prevent him from going. This morning was no different. "Someone must hunt for our dinner," Ollin had said, "And you need to perfect your spell of invisibility. There will be plenty of other opportunities for you to see the city." "Yes, sir," Matzin had replied dejectedly. He knew better than to argue with his father. So, shortly after his father had left in the form of an eagle, he had slung his quiver of arrows over his shoulder, grabbed his bow, and left the house in search of prey that continued to elude him.

He was shaken from his thoughts by the faint sound of singing. He instinctively reached for an arrow and inserted it in his bow as he carefully surveyed the immediate area. Nothing. As he listened more closely, Matzin surmised that the sound was coming from farther upstream, around a bend. He started to walk quietly in that direction. Tez paddled over to the bank of the stream and scurried onto dry land to follow Matzin. Swimming upstream in his tired state was out of the question.

"Oh gods," Tez complained, "In Your infinite wisdom there must be some reason why you chose me, an amphibian who prefers to travel at night, to protect a young boy who thinks nothing of walking for hours under a hot sun. Is this punishment for a crime I have no memory of?"

But despite the salamander's grumblings, Tez knew he would not trade places with anyone. He had grown quite fond of the boy and was not too modest to admit that he felt the gods had chosen well. Hadn't he saved the boy numerous times from injury and certain death? Yes, he was the right animal for the job, no doubt about it. Buoyed by this pep talk, he scurried from log to log, keeping one eye on Matzin and the other eye on anything that might want him for a snack.

As Matzin approached the bend in the stream he dropped to his hands and knees and crawled through the tall rushes along the bank, desiring to remain hidden until he could see who was making this melodious sound. Moments later, Matzin saw that the owner of this voice was even lovelier than the sound coming from her. For there, on the opposite bank, was a young girl picking berries from the wild bushes that grew along the edge of the stream and placing them in a large woven basket near her feet. The sun caught the golden highlights in her otherwise nut-brown hair that hung in loose curls to the middle of her back. Her smooth bronzed skin contrasted with the dazzling white of her skirt and overhanging blouse. She clearly came from a family of some importance for her ears were adorned with gold dangling earrings and two thin gold bracelets inlaid with precious stones encircled her slim wrists. And although Matzin understood most of the words of her song, her voice had an accent that he had never heard before.

"For goodness sake, he might as well be a salamander if he's not going to use his eyelids," Tez said to himself as he looked up at Matzin in disbelief. "How strange! You would think he had never seen another human before. Well, I'm not complaining. Stare away, my boy, and give your bodyguard a well-deserved rest." Tez crawled under a large leaf where he could keep an eye on the boy and yet remain hidden. However, the warm sun and exertion had taken its toll on the little salamander and he promptly fell asleep.

Matzin was oblivious to anything save the vision before

him. Although he was hot and thirsty and the stream looked inviting he dared not move for fear that he would frighten the girl and cause her to run away. Then, he had a marvelous idea. What a perfect opportunity to practice the spell of invisibility! He looked around to determine the dominant characteristic of the area so he could assume its attributes and become invisible. He finally decided upon the tall rushes that bordered the stream. He studied them intently, then stood and started to ever so slightly sway with his eyes fixed upon the girl to see if his spell worked.

Without looking up from her berry-picking, Yopica, or Pica as she was called by her friends and family, placed her hand upon the hilt of the dagger she kept tucked in the embroidered belt tied around her waist. It was hidden from view by the blouse, which hung over her skirt.

She had noticed the tall, lean boy as soon as he had come around the bend but he seemed to be alone and she thought it best to ignore him as long as he wasn't bothering her. But now he was acting strange, swaying as if possessed by demons and staring at her as if hypnotized. He was definitely not from her small village of Tacuba, where everyone knew everyone else, much to her chagrin sometimes. He came from the direction of Tenochtitlan and, therefore, was most likely an Aztec.

Pica got a tighter grip on her weapon. She had heard terrible stories of mighty Aztec warriors who swept through village after village, in the name of their Emperor, leaving only carnage and destruction behind, searching for victims to appease their Sun God. Survivors were forced to either assimilate into the Aztec Empire or perish. If this intruder even attempted to claim her as a sacrificial victim, she would kill him or die trying. But for now, it was important that she pretend not to notice him. She might need the element of surprise in her favor.

Matzin was ecstatic. The spell had worked beautifully. She hadn't noticed him at all. His father would be so proud!

He watched her delicate fingers as they picked the ripe berries. Soon the basket was full and the girl crouched down to pick it up and place it on her head. As she kneeled with her back to him, it took all of Matzin's self-control not to gasp aloud. For there, on the bottom of her right foot, was a purplish birthmark, similar to his, only smaller. Matzin felt an immediate affinity to the girl and wished there were a way to approach her without scaring her. But instead, he continued to sway as she lifted the heavy basket on to her head, held it with one hand, stood and walked away with her other hand tucked under her blouse.

As she disappeared, Matzin heard a rustling behind him. He slowly reached down, grabbed his bow, and turned to find himself no more than three body lengths from a wild turkey. He expertly inserted an arrow, released it, and killed the turkey in one try. Tez awoke to Matzin whooping with joy and exclaiming, "Now I can go home and we can have delicious grilled turkey for the evening meal! Ama will be so pleased with this rare treat. That girl brought good luck. I'll have to come back here again." Matzin slung the big bird over his back and swaggered towards home, turning once to make sure Tez was keeping up.

CHAPTER SEVENTEEN

The sun had not yet risen over the temple walls but Axolo was wide-awake, proudly reliving the events of the past few months, as if savoring a fine cup of chocolatl. His rigorous training with the jaguar knights had paid off. Within weeks, they had given him the privilege of joining them in battle. He could still hear the deafening cries of the soldiers and the howling of conch shells as the Aztec army confronted their enemies in the neighboring village.

The warriors who specialized in archery and javelin throwing had led the charge, followed by soldiers carrying obsidian-tipped swords and wooden shields. Axolo had been chosen to be one of the latter. He had felt his stomach contract into a tight knot of fear when he was first thrown into the melee of fighting where he was surrounded by piles of bloody corpses, the stench of which made him gag. But he forced himself to instead focus on the capture of each enemy soldier as a means to achieve his goals of glory, power and revenge. After that, he was invincible. Within minutes, Axolo had captured his first enemy single-handedly, which was unheard of in one so young. Before the sun had set, the Aztecs had reached the enemies' temple and burned the sanctuary of their tribal god, forcing surrender.

Returning triumphantly to the city, the Aztec soldiers marched to the palace and proudly displayed the enemies who had been captured, either to be sold as slaves or sacrificed to appease the voracious appetite of the Sun God. The Emperor was clearly pleased, especially when the commander regaled him with stories of Axolo's bravery and prowess on the battlefield. He added that in his ten years as commander, he had never seen a novice warrior fight with such tenacity and determination. "The Aztec people should praise the gods that the heir to the throne is such a fine warrior," he had exclaimed, as the soldiers murmured their assent. To receive such high praise in front of his father had been intoxicating.

Then, the commander had motioned for Axolo to approach him. When Axolo was within an arm's length, the commander had grabbed him by the hair, yanked his head back, drew his sword and brought it down quickly, slicing through the long, black lock of hair that hung down Axolo's back. Lifting the hair high above his head, the commander shouted, "The locks of boyhood have been cut. Axolo has taken another face. There now stands before you a mature warrior who has captured his first enemy in battle. I have every reason to believe that in future battles Axolo will continue to bring honor to his family and to his Empire."

And, Axolo thought with a smile, as he relived the incredible moment, that is exactly what I have done. Each successive battle had won him even more accolades and privileges, in return for only a few scars. He had now taken more than four captives with his sword, which entitled him to wear a fine, gold lip plug in the form of a serpent, and a spectacularly embroidered, fringed breechclout.

However, today he would not be wearing either of these. Today he would be challenging one of the other jaguar knights in a game of "Tlachtli," the ball game. He had yet to lose a match and he didn't anticipate today being any different. Over his loincloth he pulled a heavy leather belt. Then, into a large cotton sack he placed the rest of his protective gear, all of which he would wear when he reached the ball court.

Glancing around the room to make sure he hadn't forgotten anything, he noticed that his good luck charm, the owl, was sleeping peacefully in the corner of his room after having just returned from her nightly foraging, as evidenced by the dead rat lying at her feet.

"Sleep as long as you like, my nighttime friend,. Skill, not luck, is all that will be needed today," he said as he strutted confidently from the room. "And I have plenty of both."

****

Matzin could not contain his excitement. The day had finally come. He was going to see the city. Ollin had to buy some supplies and had asked Matzin to accompany him. They would even have an opportunity to watch a Tlachtli game between two elite warriors before returning home.

Matzin had to force himself not to gulp down the maize porridge Ama had placed before him. He didn't want to do anything that would make his father change his mind. Matzin was ignorant of the fact that he was only being included in this outing because the Rain God had appeared to Ollin in a vision last night thundering, "The time for the boy to become familiar with the city he shall inherit has come. Leave tomorrow. Do not delay or there will be grave consequences!" Ollin and Ama had no choice but to obey.

"Matzin, it is time to leave. Make sure you wear your new, white cloak for it is quite cool today," Ollin advised, "And bring your leather pouch in case I need you to carry something for me on the way home."

Tez heaved a sigh of relief. When he had heard them discussing their trip to the city he had panicked. It would have been impossible to keep up with Matzin on such a long journey. But hearing that Matzin would be bringing his leather pouch gave him an idea. He scurried over to the pouch that was lying next to Matzin's mat and scooted inside just before Matzin picked it up, drew the drawstring tight and tied it around his waist.

"It's hard to believe that it will soon be winter again. Why is it that the older I get the faster the seasons pass?" Ama mused.

"And yet you're still as lovely as the day I met you," Ollin remarked lovingly, caressing her cheek.

Ama laughed. "You better pick up a potion to aid your eyesight while you're in the city. I fear you're going blind, my love." Then, she turned her head and kissed his hand. Matzin was amazed and sometimes embarrassed that his parents were still so affectionate at their age. He quickly tied the cloak around his neck, grateful that the drop in temperature required it. His parents, of course, had repeatedly assured him that the birthmark on his arm was a blessing since it guaranteed he would never be sacrificed to the gods. But he was still self-conscious about the purplish stain and would prefer not to endure the curious looks of strangers during his first trip to the capital city.

After leaving the protection of the forest, Ollin and Matzin walked companionably along the causeway that led to Tenoch-titlan. The city was on a large island that from this distance seemed to be floating in the middle of the large, deep, blue lake that surrounded it, moored only to land by three causeways. Tez was oblivious to the scenery for not only was it pitch black inside the pouch, but the rhythm of Matzin's gait had lulled the salamander to sleep. Matzin had not been surprised by the weight of his pouch for he had seen his amphibious friend scurry inside. He was happy to have his companion along for the ride.

Soon, they reached the "chinampas," small rectangular plots of land that the Aztec farmers cultivated along the canals.

Matzin had heard of these chinampas from his parents and had been taught to have great respect for these farmers. Without their backbreaking efforts, many crops and plants would be unavailable to the Aztec people. It was not just a matter of tilling the soil. These farmers had to create their plots out of swampland. The sides of these plots were held together by wooden stakes and branches and then continually filled with canal mud, marsh weeds, and manure, to prevent them from reverting to swamp land. Watching a farmer standing waist deep in the muddy canal water cutting large, leafy weeds to place in his chinampa, Matzin was relieved that his destiny lay elsewhere.

Passing the last of the chinampas, they entered one of the outer lying calpollis, or suburbs, of the city. Here, the causeway was crowded with travelers, and the lake was filled with canoes, even though it was still early in the morning. Matzin marveled at the drawbridges on the causeway that could be raised to let the canoes pass through. Many of the canoes were paddled by merchants and farmers bringing their wares to the great marketplace in the city. Matzin gazed at the variety of goods piled high in these boats, such as precious jewels, live snakes and turtles, seashells, flowers of many varieties, stone, wood and various weapons.

"How will these merchants and farmers carry all of their wares to market once their boats have reached the outskirts of the city?" Matzin asked.

"The city is crisscrossed with a geometrical network of canals, six major ones running through the city from north to south, and two major ones running from east to west," Ollin replied. "This way, the canoes can travel almost anywhere in the city, bringing their goods directly to the marketplace faster than we could travel there by foot."

"Next time we come to the city could we come by canoe?" Matzin asked expectantly, thinking how fun it would be to navigate a vessel through the crowded canals.

"We'll see," replied Ollin.

As they passed through the calpollis and approached the center of Tenochtitlan, the houses became more luxurious. The one-story, flat-roofed mud dwellings gave way to two-story, whitewashed stucco homes surrounded by well-tended gardens. Ollin told Matzin that only noblemen and their families were allowed to live in these two-story homes. When Matzin asked him why these larger houses had no exterior windows, Ollin explained that these homes were constructed around an internal courtyard and garden, with all of the rooms having a view of this internal beauty instead of the busy pathway and canal outside. Matzin soon admired their foresight. He was so used to his humble, quiet home in the forest, that he was starting to get a headache from the cacophony of sounds in this busy city.

"There must be thousands of people here," Matzin shouted above the din.

"Actually, hundreds of thousands," Ollin replied, smiling at Matzin's astonishment.

They continued on, passing open-air stalls where merchants hawked their wares. Seeing stalls overflowing with mouth-watering things to eat, Matzin suddenly realized he was starving. As if reading his mind, Ollin stopped and said, "You must be hungry. Since this is your first visit to the city, let's splurge a little. What would you like to try?" Matzin would have liked to try a little bit of everything but he finally chose freshly-baked fish wrapped in maize husks, and a tamale. Ollin, who had decided on two tamales, paid the merchant six cacao beans. They squatted on the side of the path to eat. After the first couple of bites, Matzin felt much better, and remembering his tag-along friend, he surreptitiously squashed a beetle on the side of the road and slipped it into his pouch for the salamander.

Although he would have thought it was impossible, the

pathway and canals became even more crowded as they finished their snack. Matzin saw men, dressed only in loincloths, carrying loads of twigs on their backs with the aid of a "mecapal," or forehead strap, and women, with their faces painted with yellow ochre, balancing on their head woven baskets filled with fruits and vegetables. And directly across from where they were sitting, two men were sitting cross-legged on either side of a mat. They were playing "patolli," the popular dice game. Unlike the ball game Tlatchli, patolli could be played by commoners and nobles alike. Matzin's parents had taught him to play when he was younger but had cautioned him from playing it in the city, where patolli was a gambling game, and seasoned players could easily steal the cape off your shoulders if you weren't careful.

"Could we go over and watch a little bit of the patolli game, Father?" Matzin asked. Ollin glanced at the sun's location, then answered, "Just for a little while. The ball game will start soon, and I want to get good seats." Without giving Ollin a chance to change his mind, Matzin dodged through the throng of pedestrians to the other side of the path. Onlookers and gamblers crowded around the patolli mat, some waiting to play, others placing bets. As Matzin watched, one of the players threw the five dice, which were actually beans with numbers painted on them. He rolled a seven. He moved red-painted pebbles along the squares drawn on the large 'X' in the middle of the mat. Matzin was dumbfounded at what the onlookers were betting on the game: golden necklaces, fine turquoise, precious quetzal feathers, and beautifully-embroidered capes.

"These gamblers are willing to bet cherished objects on the unpredictable roll of a die," Ollin whispered to Matzin in a tone of disgust. "Heed my advice, son. Avoid such gambling; it only leads to ruin. A man's self-esteem does not come from receiving something merely by chance with no effort made on his part. It comes, instead, from learning an honorable craft, defending your people, and assisting fellow Aztecs in need. In doing these things you will make yourself pleasant to the gods."

"Yes, sir," Matzin replied automatically, but he was so engrossed in the game that Ollin doubted whether his son had even heard him. Putting his arm around his shoulder, he gently but firmly led him away from the mat saying, "It's time to go to the ball game now."

"Do people bet such lavish things on the outcome of the ball game as well?" Matzin asked.

"Yes," Ollin replied, "and they are to be pitied, for many of them lose not only their cloaks, but also their homes. However, the ball players are a class apart. They spend many hours practicing and they are very skilled. As you know, all of them must be of noble birth, but most are also Aztec warriors who have captured many enemies in battle. They are to be revered and respected. Sometimes the high priest himself will request a ball game, and use it as a form of fortune-telling with a future course of events assigned to each team."

"Did the high priest request today's game?" Matzin asked.

"No. It is not very common. The last one I remember was long before you were born."

At an intersection with another wide, straight footpath, they turned left towards the main temple precinct and, suddenly, the massive twin pyramids seemed to loom over them as they reached the high stone wall surrounding the sacred compound. The pyramids were crowned by vividly colored sanctuaries, red for the Sun God, blue for the Rain God, and topped with banners of precious feathers. The light of the sun, rising over the tip of the Sun God's temple, filtered through the clouds of incense escaping from the sanctuaries into the bright blue sky. The imposing wall was at least three times

Matzin's height, with carved-stone serpent heads all along the top.

"We've come to watch the ball game," Ollin said to one of the soldiers guarding the gate that was built into the wall.

"You and everyone else," replied the guard as he waved them through.

As they entered the compound, Matzin was entranced by the more than fifty buildings enclosed within. They were even more glorious than his parents had described them. The twin temple pyramid, of course, dominated the area, but he also saw priests and students entering what must be the calmecac building, and straight ahead was the imposing skull rack where the skulls of sacrificial victims were displayed. He turned his head quickly from the gruesome sight.

"This way, Matzin," Ollin said, pointing to the large white-washed building on their left. After entering the stadium, they climbed up what seemed like hundreds of stairs until they reached the viewing platform at the top. It was already very crowded, but Ollin managed to find them a good place to sit. Looking down, Matzin saw the large 'I'-shaped court with two elaborately carved stone rings mounted vertically across from each other on the center of the side walls. Suddenly, the crowd erupted as the two players walked onto the court.

"Often the game is played between two teams, but today two elite warriors are battling each other one-on-one," Ollin explained. And what magnificent warriors they were, thought Matzin. The tall, bronzed, muscular men were already wearing their protective gear; knee caps, a wide leather belt, chin pieces, half-masks covering their cheeks, and leather gloves.

"The warriors seem to wear more equipment playing this game than they do when they fight our enemies in battle," Matzin whispered to his father somewhat disdainfully.

"In my opinion, they don't protect themselves nearly

enough," Ollin replied sadly, to Matzin's surprise. "The rubber ball they propel back and forth is small but solid. More players than I can count have been mortally wounded when it has struck them in an unprotected area, such as their stomach. They also incur terrible bruises and lacerations from smashing up against the side walls or throwing themselves on the ground to get the ball. It is certainly not a game for cowards...." Ollin's last words were drowned out by loud applause and cheering from the spectators. The game had begun.

CHAPTER EIGHTEEN

Axolo deftly turned his back towards the ball that was coming toward him at great speed and used his buttocks to propel it toward the small opening in his opponent's stone ring, hoping that it would go through and he would automatically win the match. But, instead, the ball ricocheted off the edge of the ring and his opponent struck it with his knee, sending the ball back towards Axolo's ring.

Both players were so talented that they had been playing for an hour and the ball had yet to touch the ground. Axolo knew that he and the other warrior had both scored many points for performing difficult maneuvers, but Axolo still had a slight lead. The ball had slammed into him so many times that his body was covered with black and blue bruises, but for now he was able to block out the pain. He was focused only on winning.

The ball came at him and instead of trying for the ring, he launched the ball directly at the other warrior who, not expecting this unusual move, did not react quickly enough. The hard ball struck him directly in the ribs and he fell to the ground, moaning in pain. When it was clear that he could not rise unaided, two priests carried him off the court so that he could be examined and cared for. Axolo barely paid attention to his ailing opponent. All that mattered was that he was still unbeaten. He took off his mask and chin pieces and waved them in the air, basking in the adulation of the crowd cheering, "Hail Axolo, the finest of warriors! Long live the heir to the throne!"

Ollin was shocked when the champion's face was revealed, for it was the same boy who months earlier had been crying over the fate of his owl. Then, hearing the cheers of the crowd, he was stunned to learn that the champion was also one of the Emperor's sons, and, therefore, Matzin's blood brother.

"Oh gods, protect Matzin," he prayed quietly, "I have seen with my own eyes that this warrior, Axolo, has endured pain while at the calmecac that has hardened his heart. He seems to only care about another's suffering if that suffering affects him adversely, as in the case of the owl. Further, Axolo seems convinced that he shall be the next ruler of our great Empire.

"Gods, I know that you are all-knowing and have decreed that it shall be Matzin who shall replace Emperor Toltec on the throne, but today, seeing this heartless, broad-shouldered, accomplished warrior, I fear for my son's life when the truth becomes known."

Ollin then draped his arm over Matzin's shoulder as if to shield him from future events.

"Did you enjoy the game, son?"

"Yes and no," Matzin replied hesitatingly. "Watching the amazing ball-handling skills of the two players was incredible. But it seemed wrong for the winner to gloat over his victory while his opponent lay bleeding on the ground. I would have at least walked over to make sure that the other player was going to be all right. Was the winner's behavior customary?"

Ollin beamed with pride at his son's empathetic response. "No, Matzin. Not at all. I found it quite offensive, as well. It's admirable to try to beat your opponent, but it's equally important to be a gracious winner. Remember that my son."

Tez, who had watched the game from the rim of Matzin's pouch, was still unable to believe what he had just witnessed. Grown men throwing a hard round object at each other, surrounded by a crowd of people enjoying this spectacle. Didn't humans have better things to do with their time? Thankfully, Matzin wasn't interested in participating in such a ridiculous sport.

Walking back through the city, Ollin stopped at various stalls to pick up the supplies he needed. His last stop was at a stall overflowing with beautiful jewelry, where he splurged and bought a stunning gold bracelet encircled with bloodstones for Ama.

****

Weeks after his trip to the city, Matzin's body was covered with cuts and bruises but he was bound and determined to get his ball through the ring. Ollin had recently cured a nobleman from a horrible skin rash. The nobleman had been understandably surprised when Ollin had asked if the nobleman could get him an old, used Tlachtli ball in exchange for his services. The noblemen, pleased that he didn't have to pay the normal fee, immediately sent his servant out to find the requested item. An hour later, Ollin was on his way home, whistling to himself, with the ball in a sack slung over his back. Matzin was ecstatic. The ring looked authentic too, Matzin thought, thanks to his father, who had carved a small hole into a piece of stone and mounted it on the interior wall of the food shed. Ama had graciously agreed to let Matzin empty out the shed each day to practice his ball-handling skills, as long as he returned everything to its proper place by nightfall, and continued to complete his daily chores.

Tez was disgusted with the whole thing. Here he was, doing his best to protect Matzin from external forces, but he couldn't protect the boy from his own stupidity. The salamander didn't dare enter the shed while Matzin was busy mutilating himself with the wildly, bouncing round object, for fear of getting himself killed. For where would Matzin be without his loyal protector?

Just then, Matzin threw open the shed door yelling, "I did it! I got it through the ring!"

"Congratulations," replied Ama, who was kneeling near the hut grounding herbs, "Your hard work has paid off."

For heaven's sake, don't encourage the boy, thought Tez, exasperated, and he watched in disbelief as Matzin reentered the shed and closed the door behind him.

CHAPTER NINETEEN

Axolo displaced the reflection of the moon with his oar as he paddled away from the city towards the snow-capped mountains. Although it was early spring, he was thankful for his new jaguar-skin cape because the air was still quite cold. Off to his left he saw a flotilla of magnificent vessels navigating their way toward Mount Tlaloc. The flat-bottomed barges were decorated with red cotton awnings and on one of them was a large box. Even though the boats were too far away to identify anyone on them, Axolo knew that his father was seated in the lead vessel with the high priest, Kan, while the Aztec lords and their servants occupied the boats that followed.

Omo, the owl, flew alongside the canoe wondering what Axolo was up to now. She hoped that it was something that could be accomplished in a short time, because it would soon be daybreak and then she would be of no help at all. She really did not understand why she, a nocturnal animal, had been put in charge of the future Emperor of this vast Aztec kingdom. But it was not her place to question the gods' decisions. So, she continued trailing Axolo's canoe, which took him toward the mountainous forests.

Soon, Axolo reached the shore. He picked up strips of thick maguey rope, his knife, bow and quiver of arrows from the bottom of the canoe, leapt out and pulled the vessel onto the beach. He averted his eyes from the hateful maguey plant as he walked towards the dense forest. The rich colors of the forest sprang to life as the sun started to rise above the mountaintops. Omo tried to force herself to stay awake, but it was no use. She was too tired. She decided to return to the canoe and perch inside the vessel. That way, when Axolo returned, which she hoped would be soon and safely, she would awaken and accompany him back to the city.

As Axolo climbed the mountain, he congratulated himself on being chosen to undertake this important mission. Each spring, the Emperor, his lords and the high priest traveled to Mount Tlaloc with one of the recently captured enemy prisoners. This captive was placed in an enclosed litter and carried by servants up the sacred mountain. Upon reaching the peak, the venerable group of men waited, sometimes for days, until Tlaloc, the Rain God, sent a thunderstorm. This was the sign for the sacrificial ceremony to begin. The enemy was released from the litter and slain by the high priest accompanied by the sound of conch shells and wooden flutes. Upon completion of the mountain sacrifice, the vessels returned to the city. Meanwhile, a girl needed to be captured from a neighboring tribe and dressed in blue to represent the water graciously provided by the Rain God. She would then be imprisoned in the sanctuary of Tlaloc's temple in the main temple precinct. As soon as the returning barges were sighted, the girl would be enclosed in a litter and placed in a canoe. Warriors would paddle the canoe to the middle of the lake and cast the litter overboard, completing the annual spring sacrifices to Tlaloc.

This was where Axolo came in. It was his job to capture a girl and bring her back to the temple before the Emperor's vessel returned.

As he reached the higher elevations, Axolo heard the sound of rushing water and realized that he was quite thirsty. He walked towards the sound and soon came upon a stream. Kneeling down, he scooped the icy-cold water into his mouth, then froze as he heard a high-pitched fluctuating noise over the sound of the gushing stream. It seemed to come from around the bend up ahead. Holding his knife, he crouched and walked quietly through the rushes along the bank to see who or what was making that sound.

****

Ama watched her son as he grabbed his bow and slung his quiver of arrows over his shoulder. She couldn't believe that the baby boy that had fit into the crook of her arm was now a fine, young man, taller than both of his parents.

"I'm going hunting, Mother. Don't wait for me if I'm not back for the midday meal!" Matzin said, and then he raced outside.

"Be careful! "she yelled after him wondering why Matzin was in such a hurry. For the past couple of months he had been the first one up and before she and Ollin had even finished their morning meal, Matzin had finished his chores and was preparing to leave. When he returned, many hours later, he usually had a sack full of fresh kill for which Ama was thankful, but he also had a goofy grin on his face and a dreamy look in his eyes, which made Ama suspicious. But before she ever had a chance to question him, he would lock himself in the food shed to practice with the Tlachtli ball, with which he was becoming quite skilled.

Today, Ollin was in the city on business, and Ama had nothing to do that couldn't be put off until tomorrow. Dying of curiosity, she decided to follow Matzin to see what was making him act so strangely. But it was important that Matzin not notice her or he would think that she did not trust him, which would be a disaster. A spell of transformation should do the trick, she decided. Although Ollin used this spell quite often, it had been quite a while since Ama had felt the need to transform herself into another creature. She hoped that she wouldn't have any trouble. Now, what should she become? Certainly not a jaguar or a large bird, or anything else that Matzin might look upon as prey. She finally decided upon a snake. This way she could move quickly through the forest but could also remain hidden so as not to attract Matzin's attention. Minutes later, the hut was empty and a long, thin snake, ringed in green and gold was quickly slithering in the direction of the stream.

****

Pica had nearly filled her basket with berries and was surprised to find that she was disappointed that the strange, swaying boy had not yet come. Ever since the first day that she had seen him, the boy had arrived shortly after she did and watched her from the other side of the stream, silently swaying like a reed. She had grown used to having this boy around and in a strange way felt safer when he was there. However, today, Pica had arrived at the stream earlier than usual because her village was having a special spring celebration at sundown. She had to pick the berries quickly and return home to help prepare for the festivities.

With a sigh, she knelt to get another handful of berries, and as she stood up was startled to find that the boy had appeared at the edge of the stream as if by magic. He is either getting quite good at moving noiselessly through the forest, Pica thought, or I am getting too caught up in my daydreams and not paying enough attention to my surroundings.

"I have to be more vigilant," she reprimanded herself, "For although the swaying boy doesn't seem dangerous, other creatures in the forest are."

She patted her thigh to make sure that her knife was still there.

Once Ama turned the bend in the stream and saw the beautiful white-clothed girl, everything became ridiculously clear. And as she watched her son performing what appeared to be a bizarre mating dance among the reeds, she realized that she and Ollin had been so busy preparing their son to be king, that they had woefully neglected to teach him how to woo a potential queen. Fortunately, this lovely girl seemed to have the grace and good manners not to laugh uproariously at Matzin's antics, but she certainly wasn't going to regard him as a potential suitor. Ama would have to take care of this matter as soon as possible. As Ama looked at the beautiful girl more closely, she noticed that the embroidery on her white blouse and ankle-length skirt contained lovely patterns not found on an Aztec woman's clothing. This girl must belong to one of the neighboring villages, Ama thought. However, based on her exquisite jewelry, the girl was also clearly of noble birth. Realizing by the hypnotized look on her son's face that she might be there awhile, Ama slithered next to a warm rock, careful to remain out of Matzin's sight. She decided to enjoy the sunshine and relax a little before returning to the hut to start preparing the midday meal.

****

From inside a hollow log, at the edge of the stream, Tez spied the long, gold and green ringed snake. At first, Tez was paralyzed with fear but felt slightly less nauseous when he realized that the snake was motionless and didn't seem to notice the trembling salamander.

"Nevertheless," Tez said to himself, "Looks can be deceiving. That evil serpent might just be trying to lure me into a false sense of security. And I will be of no use to Matzin if I become the morning meal for that slimy monster."

Tez backed slowly to the other end of the log, keeping his eyes on the snake. When he reached the opening at the other end, he turned and silently scurried farther upstream, and then up a tree, putting as much distance between him and the snake as he could while still being able to keep an eye on Matzin. As he reached the tree's upper branches, he stopped to catch his breath and looked down. He was relieved to see that the snake had not moved and pleased that from this vantage point he could easily watch over his charge. He would have to watch out for other predators, like birds, but no one said the life of a salamander was going to be easy. Just then, a distant dark shape caught Tez's eye. As the shape moved closer, the sun glinted off a metal object, temporarily blinding the salamander. When Tez could see again, he realized that the shape had taken the form of a bronzed, young man who was moving stealthily toward the stream. The stranger neared the edge of the water, got on his belly, and silently crawled into the tall reeds. He held a sharp-tipped knife in one hand and strips of rope in the other, and seemed to be interested in the same girl Matzin had been spying on for weeks.

Fortunately, the stranger had arrived at the stream by way of a different path through the forest than the one Matzin had taken and was not yet aware of the boy swaying among the reeds further downstream. But it was only a matter of time before Matzin's ridiculous antics would catch the stranger's attention, thought Tez. And then what? Tez decided that he had better get closer to the stranger to distract him, if necessary. Keeping his eye on the snake, which seemed to be asleep, Tez scurried down the tree and took off in the direction of the bronzed, young man, fervently praying that the hateful serpent didn't have any friends nearby.

A low, rumbling from his stomach reminded Matzin that it had been a long time since he had last eaten. His mouth was dry as well. Trying his best to imitate a reed gently falling to the ground, he gyrated to a sitting position and reached into his leather pouch for the tortilla that he had hurriedly placed there this morning. After taking a few bites, he quietly reached through the reeds with both hands cupped, filled them with water from the cool stream and bent to drink. Suddenly there was a loud, piercing scream, then another. Matzin leaped up and was horrified to see that a large man had grabbed the girl from behind. She was thrashing about wildly, like a fish after being caught, but her struggles were clearly in vain against such a strong opponent. Matzin quickly pulled an arrow from his quiver and placed it in his bow. As he took careful aim to wound the intruder without hurting the girl, he gasped in disbelief and dropped his bow. The abductor was none other than the elite warrior who had cockily triumphed at the ball game. Matzin knew he would bring down the wrath of the gods upon the Aztec people if he harmed an Aztec warrior. So, he watched helplessly in agony as the warrior bound the girl's legs and arms with rope and laid her on the bank of the stream. Then, with his back to the screaming, writhing girl, the warrior leaned against a tree, took out some food from a cloth sack, and proceeded to eat.

Matzin wracked his brain for a way to save the girl without harming the warrior. Then it hit him. He was still under the spell of invisibility. Continuing to take on the characteristics of the swaying reeds, he moved further upstream. He hoped to quickly free the girl from the ropes so that she could at least try to escape before the warrior finished his meal.

****

Axolo was pleased with himself. Clearly the gods continued to shower blessings upon him, the chosen one. How many warriors could boast of capturing the Rain God's female sacrifice so quickly, and such a beautiful one at that? He was eager to return to the city with his prize and see the look of pride on his father's face. He finished the last bite of his tortilla, slung his bow and quiver over his shoulder, tucked his knife in his loincloth and stood up. He stretched his arms over his head, turned toward the bound girl, and immediately froze in disbelief. An impudent young fool was brazenly walking through the reeds towards the girl, for what purpose one could only guess. Well, walking wasn't quite an accurate description. The fool was swaying with his arms above his head as he moved upstream. Axolo did not hesitate; no one was going to ruin this day for him, especially a crazy lunatic. He fit an arrow to his bow. It felt heavier than usual but he didn't have time to figure out why. He set the boy in his sights, pulled back on the string and then let go. The boy screamed in agony and then collapsed among the reeds. Axolo didn't wait around to see if the boy was dead or not. All that mattered was that the stranger was no longer an impediment to his plans. He walked over to the sobbing girl, slung her over his shoulder and carried her back in the direction from which he had come.

****

Ama, now in her human form, pulled a purplish-black powder from her leather pouch, and spit on it repeatedly until it became paste-like. Then, she rubbed the mixture on Matzin's ankle as she repeated an incantation seven times. She stroked her son's head as tears streamed down her face. She could not escape the fact that by trying to protect her son she might have killed him. And she began to sob convulsively as her mind replayed the last few minutes over and over again…

The girl's screams had startled Ama from her slumber and when she saw her son fit an arrow in his bow, she quickly slithered up the nearest tree to see what was going on. She was startled to see a muscular, young man attacking the pretty girl. However, then she noticed the shorn hair and the flagellation marks on his back. And when she recalled what day it was, she understood with a sinking heart what was happening. An Aztec warrior was capturing the sacrifice for today's ceremony in honor of Tlaloc, the Rain God. She knew that Tlaloc would be extremely pleased with such a perfect sacrifice but her son would be heartbroken. It was moments like these that made being a parent one of the hardest jobs she had ever had.

Fortunately, it seemed her son had recognized the man as an Aztec warrior, for he had dropped his bow on the ground. Then, she heard Matzin quietly exclaim, "That's right! I'm still under the spell of invisibility!" And he started moving towards the girl. Ama realized that although she and Ollin had described the Mount Tlaloc ceremony to Matzin during one of his lessons years ago, there was no reason why her son would connect these two events. Therefore, not knowing it was a sacred rite, her son would do anything to rescue the girl he had grown so fond of, short of harming the warrior. Knowing full well that her son could not actually perform the invisibility spell, and that an Aztec warrior would resent any interference with his duties, Ama slithered down the tree and followed her son through the reeds. When she saw that the warrior was aiming an arrow at her son's heart, she took the only course of action left to her. She sprang at her son with her fangs bared and bit deeply into his ankle releasing deadly venom into his bloodstream. Matzin screamed and immediately collapsed just as the arrow inexplicably fell just short of its mark.

Ama knew that she didn't have a moment to lose. She quickly transformed herself back to her natural state, and began preparing the only known antidote to such a deadly snakebite. It had to be applied within minutes to the puncture wound to be effective. Fortunately, the warrior, correctly believing that Matzin was no longer a threat, never glanced their way again. As she worked feverishly, Ama saw the Aztec pick up the girl and stride away into the forest. And now here she sat, praying to all the gods in the heavens to help her save her son. During her ministrations, she had no reason to notice the little salamander lying motionless next to the recently released arrow.

****

Tez slowly looked around, fearful of what he might find. He didn't know how long he had been unconscious but it felt like every part of his little spotted body was bruised and battered. He was amazed that he had even survived at all after what he had just been through. He had moved right to the feet of the stranger after he saw the horrible things he had done to the pretty girl. This stranger was dangerous and Matzin might need the salamander's help. Then, he saw Matzin approaching the girl, who was desperately trying to free herself from the tight ropes. He was completely unarmed and walking in a bizarre fashion with his arms raised above his head while his hips swayed back and forth.

"This is no time to show off your silly dances, you imbecile!" thought Tez. It was times like these when he questioned the gods' selection of this boy as the next Aztec Emperor.

Tez watched in horror as the stranger removed the bow from his shoulder and reached for an arrow from his quiver. What could he do to protect Matzin this time? The stranger pulled out an arrow so forcefully that it slipped from his grasp and fell to the ground. As he reached down to pick it up, he kept his eyes on Matzin. Tez knew that if he had any hope of saving Matzin's life he had to act quickly. Without having time to think through the consequences of what he was about to do and putting all his trust in the gods to help this poor creature they had chosen to protect the future Emperor, Tez scurried into the mass of feathers attached to the end of the arrow and held on tight. He was completely hidden from sight. The stranger lifted the arrow and fit it into his bow. Tez had just enough time to hope that the added weight would make the arrow go off target. Then, all of a sudden, the little salamander was flying through the air at a speed never experienced by any salamander before or since. For a split second, it was invigorating and then the downward trajectory began. Tez braced himself for the fall. As the arrow struck the ground, Tez was flung onto the dirt next to the green and gold serpent. Just my luck, he thought, then everything went black.

CHAPTER TWENTY

By the time Axolo's canoe began to navigate the canals that crisscrossed the capital city, the sun had set behind the twin temples and the sliver of moon in the sky barely illuminated the practically empty streets. Axolo had been pleasantly surprised to find his owl sleeping in the canoe. It was as if the animal had appeared by magic. And once again, the owl had brought him luck. He had found a perfect victim in record time. His father would be so pleased! After wending his way through the canals of the city, Axolo docked his vessel and roughly slung the still-struggling girl over his shoulder. He carried her to the calmecac school, where he unceremoniously dumped her in the dirt at the feet of the captain of the Eagle Knights who had been waiting to make sure that Axolo successfully captured an acceptable female sacrifice.

Omo, who was now wide-awake, was perched on the corner of the calmecac building. Fortunately, Axolo had managed to return safely, no thanks to her. She was shocked, however, to discover that kidnapping a helpless girl was apparently something that pleased his superiors.

"She is exceptionally beautiful and unblemished, Axolo. Tlaloc, the Rain God will be pleased and so am I, for you have brought great honor to the Eagle Knights by the timely completion of your mission."

"Thank you, sir," replied Axolo, pleased with the justified

praise. "Will someone notify the high priest of my return so that he may imprison the victim in Tlaloc's temple until the Emperor's boats return?"

Axolo was surprised to see a pained, sorrowful look suddenly appear on the captain's face.

"Kan will be unable to perform his duties at the spring sacrifice to our all-mighty Rain God. Today, during the morning meal, he collapsed. Thankfully, he has regained consciousness, but he is weak and feverish and unable to even sit up without feeling dizzy. We have been praying all morning to Quetzalcoatl, the god of priests, but I must admit it does not look good."

Axolo was stunned and also angry. If Kan died during the spring sacrifices, Axolo's accomplishment would be overshadowed by funeral preparations and mourning for the high priest. That would be unacceptable after all Axolo had been through.

"I am deeply sorry to hear this sad news," Axolo replied, truthfully. "Who then shall be responsible for imprisoning this victim?"

" Teo. The high priest has been grooming Teo to succeed him so he will temporarily take over Kan's duties. He has requested that you carry the victim directly to the top of the temple steps. He will meet you there."

"Of course, sir."

Axolo once again slung the girl over his shoulder and strode off towards the twin temples. On the way, he imagined the proud look on his father's face when he returned from the mountain sacrifice to find that his son was responsible for bringing such a perfect sacrifice for Tlaloc. Axolo noticed that the girl's tears were beginning to soak through his cloak. Axolo smiled, for he knew that a victim's tears were considered a good sign, for they represented rain for the Rain God.

****

Ama had been cradling Matzin's head in her lap for hours and stroking his forehead with her lips moving silently in prayer, when all of a sudden her son's long eyelashes fluttered open.

"Oh gods be praised!" exclaimed Ama, as tears ran unchecked down her face.

"Mother! What is the matter?" Matzin asked, alarmed by his mother's tears. Looking around and seeing the waning moon overhead he tried to discern why he was lying in the middle of the forest at this time of night. Then, suddenly, reality came piercing through like a warrior's spear. He leaped up and then immediately fell to his knees as the world seemed to spin around his head and his left ankle felt as if it were on fire.

"Matzin, be still!" Ama cried, "It will be several more hours before you completely recover. Just be thankful that you are alive."

"Recovered? Recovered from what? What happened? The last thing I remember is approaching the Aztec warrior to save my...I mean... the girl, and then I collapsed." It took all the self-control drilled into him by his parents for so many years, to prevent him from becoming completely hysterical.

"Mother, you don't understand! You would have been repulsed by what I saw. A large, muscular Aztec warrior, the same one who was victorious at the ball game that Father and I attended, attacked a poor, defenseless girl in the middle of the stream. I've got to find her!" Again, he tried to stand.

"Son, you must calm down," Ama said. "I know what happened and there is a reasonable explanation for the warrior's behavior. You must listen to me."

Holding her son's hands in her own, she reminded him of the Mt. Tlaloc ceremony and the spring sacrifices that were required. Then, she explained what she had done to prevent him from interfering in this ritual. As understanding dawned, Matzin could no longer contain himself. He let out a primal scream that echoed throughout the forest as Ama sat by helplessly.

****

Tez awoke with a start. Glancing to his left, he was relieved to see that Matzin was still alive and that the slithering snake was nowhere to be seen, although Ama had inexplicably joined them. Remembering his virgin flight through the forest, the little salamander was extremely proud of himself for yet again rescuing his charge from mortal danger.

I am just one awesome, flying amphibian! he thought to himself. He cautiously moved his limbs and was relieved that although he felt like Matzin had used him as a Tlachtli ball, it didn't appear that anything was broken. However, he knew he was too weak and bruised to escape predators on the way home, so he inched his way over to Matzin's quiver and settled in among the arrows where he promptly fell to sleep.

CHAPTER TWENTY ONE

When Axolo returned to the calmecac building, he was surprised to find a group of students on the steps, huddled together and whispering amongst themselves.

One of the students saw Axolo approaching and hurried towards him.

"Have you heard the news about Kan?"

"Yes, I've heard that he is ill," Axolo responded in a disgusted tone.

"Not just ill," the student replied, "He fears that he is dying and has asked the priest, Teo, to hear his confession."

Axolo was furious at Kan's poor timing. It was as if the high priest were purposely trying to shift the attention away from Axolo's accomplishment. However, if Kan had sent for a confessor it must be serious, for, according to Aztec law, each person was allowed only one confession during his or her lifetime. Therefore, one usually waited until his or her last dying breath to confess because whatever was confessed to was not only immediately forgiven after performing a penance, but also was no longer punishable by law.

Axolo strode past the other students into the building and down the hallway towards Kan's personal quarters. He wanted to see for himself if the rumors were true. As he approached Kan's room, he heard low voices. He peeked his head around the doorway and saw Kan lying on a newly woven mat with the confessor-priest kneeling next to him on an identical mat, as was the custom. Kan's eyes were closed and his breathing was labored. Teo had his back to Axolo. Axolo could smell the pungent aroma of burning incense wafting throughout the room.

"Oh gods," the priest intoned solemnly, with an upraised face, "Behold a poor man who is weeping, sad and anxious. He comes with a heavy heart, full of sorrow. Lord, our master, make his trouble cease, pacify his heart." Then, turning towards Kan he continued, "Kan, confess sincerely to the gods. Open your heart; release all of your secrets. Do not be restrained by shame. Will you do this freely?"

"I will," responded Kan weakly. "It will be a relief to unburden my soul."

This should be interesting, thought Axolo. What could a high priest possibly have done that is so sinful? He looked up and down the corridor to make sure he was still alone in the hallway, and then continued to eavesdrop.

" Fifteen years ago, the kingdom rejoiced upon the birth of a son to Emperor Toltec and Empress Mia, a son born under a very auspicious sign. However, this is only a part of the story…"

Axolo realized that Kan was going to reveal the existence of the evil twin. But why? This had nothing to do with Kan's sins other than keeping it a secret to spare his mother and the rest of the kingdom heartache.

Kan continued, "The Empress actually gave birth to twin boys. However, I determined that the latter-born twin was born under the most unfavorable sign and was destined to become a witch."

The confessor-priest gasped in horror at this revelation.

"Your reaction was my own," Kan murmured sadly. "As you know, by law someone born under that sign has to be brought to the witches' enclave and raised by them. I was chosen to fulfill this horrendous task. Upon returning from the enclave,

I discovered that I had mistakenly deciphered the latter-born twin's birth sign. In fact, he was born under the sign 4-acatl and destined to become a courageous leader of our people."

At this point in the narrative, Kan's voice faltered as his supine body convulsed with sobs. Axolo sank to the ground and felt as if his head were going to explode. "This is not possible. He is lying!" he kept repeating to himself. But, he knew that Kan was speaking the truth. No one lied during a confession to the gods.

"Continue, Kan," whispered the astonished priest.

"Of course I hurried back to the witches' den but to my horror the baby was already gone."

Teo, for the first time in his life, was at a loss for words. The ramifications of this cataclysmic mistake by Kan were too horrendous to contemplate. However, the dying man deserved to receive his penance.

"Kan, your actions, although most likely leading to disastrous consequences for our Empire, were not intentional. Further, as soon as you discovered your mistake you tried to rectify the situation. Therefore, after receiving a scarring of your tongue, may the gods forgive you of your sins and may there finally be peace in your heart."

The priest then grasped an obsidian knife lying next to the mat. Kan opened his mouth, the priest grabbed his tongue, made three deep cuts on it and turned Kan's head to the side so the blood would drain out of the side of his mouth instead of down his throat. Teo rolled up his mat, slowly stood and turned towards the hallway. Then, turning his head back towards the dying man, he asked, "Would we ever be able to recognize this banished twin were he to return to the city?"

Kan nodded and although it was almost impossible for him to speak because of his swelling tongue, he pointed to his upper right arm and whispered, "Purple birthmark…" Then, he lost consciousness.

Axolo, realizing that Teo was about to exit the room, quickly darted into the room immediately next to Kan's and waited there in the darkness until he was sure the priest had gone. Returning to his own room, he slammed his fist into the wall repeatedly until his knuckles were bruised and bleeding, startling Omo from her sleep in the corner of the room. He was consumed with rage. All of the humiliation and punishments he had endured at school, all of the battles he had won, all of the accolades he had received would be for naught if this hateful twin somehow usurped Axolo's place as the next Emperor. Fortunately, the priest was bound to keep all confessions secret as long as the confessor was still alive, and the penalty of revealing a confession, even to the Emperor, was instant death. However, Axolo, although strong and ruthless, realized that his twin had been left with witches and, therefore, was probably capable of using black magic to get his way. Against such powerful magic, Axolo had no defense. The only course of action was to strike first before the twin could react. If that piece of garbage entered the city, Axolo would have to eliminate him before his twin took away the only thing Axolo cared about --- the crown.

CHAPTER TWENTY TWO

The Tlachtli ball had been slamming against the walls of the food shed for hours. Ama, who was inside the hut preparing tortillas, knew that her son was attempting to release some of his frustration at his inability to rescue a girl that he had evidently grown quite fond of and whom he would most likely never see again. A couple of weeks ago, Ama and Ollin had decided that they would surprise Matzin and take him to the city for the spring sacrifice, which was always followed by a sumptuous feast. Now, of course, such an outing was out of the question. Her heart ached for her son and if she could have done something to change the situation she would have done it gladly. However, it was necessary that the Rain God receive his victim. Interfering with this ritual could bring drought and famine to the entire Aztec people. She and Ollin would have to figure out a way to introduce Matzin to other young women who could hopefully, over time, help him to forget this first strong infatuation.

As she flattened the tortilla dough into flat, round circles, she reminded herself that the most important thing was that the antidote had been effective against the deadly snakebite, and that her son was alive and well. The gods were good.

****

As Tez paced back and forth in front of the shed, he

wondered if the gods were trying to make him have a nervous breakdown. Either that or they had a very warped sense of humor. Yesterday morning I became the first flying salamander, risking life and limb to deflect an arrow from piercing Matzin's heart, he thought. Today, our 'future Emperor' has spent the whole morning beating himself up with a ball. Sometimes I wonder why I even bother.

As if Matzin had heard Tez, the noises inside the shed suddenly ceased. Then, Matzin burst out of the door with a huge grin on his face. Reaching down, he scooped up the salamander and held it up to his face exclaiming, "The birthmark on the bottom of her foot! The birthmark! She's not unblemished! She can't be sacrificed! But, my little friend, we need to hurry!" With a flourish, he reached down with his free hand, picked up his leather pouch, gently placed the salamander inside, and started to run down the mountain path towards the lake.

Tez didn't have time to wonder what in the world was going on and, in fact, he didn't really care. The future Emperor of the Aztec nation had just called him his 'little friend.' Matzin obviously recognizes all that I have done for him, thought Tez, and realizes that he needs me with him at all times to provide protection! Tez curled up in the bottom of the pouch with a goofy grin on his face and decided to get some sleep before his services were needed again.

CHAPTER TWENTY THREE

Just as the calmecac students were finishing their midday meal, they heard the sound of conch shells being blown. That could mean only one thing. The Emperor's vessels were returning from the mountain sacrifice. Axolo was ecstatic! Kan had somehow survived the night and was sleeping peacefully. The priests were amazed at this turn of events, but Axolo knew it was just one more indication that the gods were on his side.

He couldn't wait to hear the warm words of praise that were sure to come from his father when Toltec saw the exquisitely beautiful victim that Axolo had captured for today's sacrifice. Right about now, thought Axolo, Teo, who had temporarily assumed Kan's duties, should be placing the girl in a litter that would be ceremoniously carried by four Jaguar Knights, one of whom would be Axolo, down the temple steps, and through the city streets to the lake's edge, where all of the inhabitants would be gathered to witness the joyous event. The litter would then be placed in a large decorated canoe and Axolo, together with the three other warriors, would paddle to the middle of the lake and dump the litter overboard as a precious gift to Tlaloc, the Rain God.

It was a great honor to be chosen to carry the litter and Axolo felt more than worthy to receive it. He quickly left the main dining hall to change into his ceremonial garb. He knew that this would be a day he would remember for the rest of his life.

As Matzin raced along the causeway towards the city he saw the flotilla of boats off to his right and heard the unmistakable sound of conch shells blowing. His legs burned from running such a long distance but he forced himself to pick up the pace, knowing that any minute now the girl would be removed from Tlaloc's sanctuary, carried to the lake and drowned. It was imperative that the high priest be told of the girl's birthmark before she was sacrificed. For the sacrifice of an imperfect victim would incur Tlaloc's wrath even more than no offering at all.

Once Matzin reached the end of the causeway, he was forced to slow down because the streets teemed with people, all of them wanting to witness this momentous event and join in the festivities afterward. Commoners in crisp, white cloaks and dignitaries in richly embroidered mantles intermingled as they strode towards the Great Pyramid. The merchants were out in full force, recognizing that this was a fabulous opportunity to hawk their wares. Matzin dodged in and out of the throng as quickly as he could and in the process just missed stepping on a merchant's basket filled to the brim with centipedes and spiders. The smell of freshly-baked tamales reminded Matzin that he hadn't eaten in a long time, but he just kept moving through the crowd. There would be time to eat later if he successfully prevented the sacrifice.

After what seemed like an eternity, he reached the wall topped with serpent carvings that surrounded the temple precinct. Just like on the day that Matzin and his father had attended the ball game, the fortified gates, although still guarded by armed warriors, were left open to allow the public to watch the victim's litter being carried down the temple steps. Matzin was relieved to see that the four warriors chosen to carry the litter had just reached the top of the pyramid. But that still didn't leave him with much time to act. As Matzin navigated his way through the mass of people towards the Great Pyramid, the sound of wooden gongs suddenly echoed throughout the courtyard.

"There's the litter! The warriors are bringing it down the steps!" someone exclaimed.

Matzin frantically began to push his way through the crowd, causing several people to make pointed remarks about his total lack of manners. He didn't care. He knew that if he didn't get the warriors' attention while they were still descending the temple steps, he would never have another chance. As soon as they reached the ground, the citizens' cheers would drown out Matzin's cries.

When the elite warriors reached the halfway point, Matzin finally burst through to the front of the crowd and then hesitated. He knew that it was against the law for anyone other than the high priest or a designated warrior to mount the temple steps. Failure to obey would lead to severe punishment and possibly banishment from the kingdom. Armed guards surrounded the base of the pyramids to enforce this law. But if he did nothing, and an imperfect victim was sacrificed to Tlaloc, death and destruction would result. Then, like a bolt of lightning, he was struck with an idea. The invisibility spell! Why hadn't he thought of this before? With no time to lose, he focused all of his energy on blending in with his environment so as to become invisible. This was a daunting task because the pyramid was nothing but a great barren block of stone and the warriors carrying the litter were now two-thirds of the way down the ...steps! Yes, steps! He would blend in with the steps by slithering up them on his belly like his little friend the salamander. Matzin dropped to the ground, and began to slowly crawl up the stairs. The crowd's upturned faces were so focused on the descending litter that they did not notice the strange young man. The soldiers guarding the base of the pyramid were looking straight ahead, not down, and, therefore, did not see that security of the perimeter had been breached. The four warriors carrying the litter were trained to never look down and so were also unaware of the approaching boy. Matzin mistook the inattention to his ascent as proof that he had once again succeeded in becoming invisible.

As he continued to climb, Matzin's leather pouch banged against the hard stone. Tez was jostled about and was not very happy about the way Matzin was treating his friend. For heaven's sake, what was the boy up to now?

****

From his vantage point on the pyramid steps, Axolo could see his father's vessel, which had just docked at the outskirts of the city. The Emperor would be awaiting the arrival of the sacrificial victim and upon seeing the exquisite beauty of the girl his son had captured, Axolo was sure to receive hearty praise. He couldn't wait.

The four warriors were now five steps away from the slithering boy. Suddenly, Matzin stood up knowing that such a sudden movement would cause him to become visible again. The crowd began to scream and the warriors, startled by his sudden appearance, nearly dropped the litter. Tez peeked from the pouch and was horrified to see at least ten armed and angry soldiers racing up the steps towards Matzin.

"How am I supposed to get Matzin out of this one?" he thought miserably.

Matzin, at first, was dumbstruck with horror because as soon as he had leapt up he had realized that one of the litter bearers was none other than the warrior who had been so heartless in the ball game and who had abducted the girl at the stream. With difficulty, he swallowed his rage and desire to rush at this cocky thug and knock him senseless. Instead, knowing time was of the essence, he raised his right arm and yelled, "Please stop! There has been a terrible mistake!"

Axolo couldn't breathe. The purple birthmark that had haunted him in his nightmares was being raised right in front of his face. His evil twin had appeared out of nowhere using some black magic spell. The confrontation he had dreaded had finally arrived. He didn't care how many tricks this witch had in his arsenal because he had worked too hard and endured too much to allow this charlatan to outsmart him.

"Seize this criminal!" Axolo shouted to the guards who had finally reached Matzin and surrounded him, "Take him away and may he receive the penalty of death for daring to break our sacred laws during this important ceremony!"

"You forget your rank, Axolo," the chief knight said harshly from the other side of the litter. "It is not up to a mere warrior, even one who is the Emperor's son, to give out such orders or dole out punishment."

Matzin was dumbstruck. The Emperor's son? This egomaniac was next in line to the throne? If true, Matzin feared for the future of the Aztec Empire. Tez was also stunned. The Emperor's son? There must be some mistake. Tez was the one the gods had put in charge of protecting the successor to the throne and that man was Matzin. Tez would just have to accept that the gods, in their infinite wisdom, had a plan that would eventually be made known. Meanwhile, his charge was in imminent danger and had to be rescued. But how? Unnoticed, Tez slithered out of the pouch and dropped to the ground.

Axolo was enraged to be chastised in public but he knew better than to argue with the chief.

"What is your name, boy?" asked the chief.

"Matzin, sir."

"Matzin, why have you done such an outrageous thing? You must know that the punishment is severe."

"Yes, sir. But I knew that if I didn't do something the

consequences for the Empire would be disastrous!"

"What are you talking about?" replied the chief, clearly mystified by this articulate, obviously well-bred boy.

"Sir, Tlaloc requires that his victims be completely unblemished, does he not?" answered Matzin.

"Of course, boy. And if you had seen this girl you would know that she is perfection itself."

"But that's just it, sir! I have seen her and she is not perfect! She has a birthmark on the bottom of her right foot."

The chief turned to Axolo with a grim look.

"If this is true Axolo, you have not only let me and your father down, but the entire Aztec Empire is now in danger. You risk not only losing your right to the crown, but being banished as well."

Axolo replied in a voice trembling with anger, "He's lying! None other than our high priest, Kan, had warned me to be on the lookout for a boy with just such a birthmark on his arm. He is a witch and is trying to do everything in his power to prevent the natural succession of power to me so that the witches of Malinalco can take over."

Matzin and Tez were shocked at Axolo's lies and the unexplained hatred of Matzin that the warrior's voice revealed.

"I am not a witch! You're the liar!" Matzin exclaimed.

"Well, there is an easy way to see who is telling the truth," said the chief, then added, "Guards! Unlock the litter and examine the bottom of the victim's feet. The litter was turned sideways and placed gingerly on the wide step. The guards unlocked the door and were about to open it when Axolo cried out, "Sir, if this witch could appear out of nowhere, surely he could use his black magic to create a birthmark where there once was none in an effort to discredit me."

The chief paused and, nodding his head, replied, "This is certainly possible, Axolo. I had not thought of it. Well, this is quite a conundrum. Guards, bind Matzin's hands, feet and mouth to prevent him from casting any spells and carry him to the water's edge. We will follow with the litter and ask the Emperor for guidance."

Tez looked up at the heavens and fervently prayed, "Oh gods, I know you have been relying on me to get Matzin out of trouble but we're a little outnumbered here today and could sure use some of your divine help."

Just as the guards started to wrap maguey rope around Matzin's hands, the sky began to darken. Looking up, the crowd saw the moon starting to cover the sun. An eclipse! Aztec law required that during an eclipse everyone must bow down, keeping his eyes to the ground, to avoid angering the Sun God. If this were not done, the sun might not come up the next day. All of the people, including the warriors, quickly knelt down with a bowed head.

Tez was ecstatic! "Do the gods listen to me or what?" he thought exultantly. Then, he was dismayed to see Matzin bowing down too.

"Get up you dolt!" Tez thought furiously, wishing not for the first time that the gods had given him the power of speech. "The gods are providing you with a miraculous means of escape. Don't miss your chance!"

Matzin knelt down, frightened and confused. If the Emperor believed Axolo's story, the girl would be sacrificed, Matzin would probably be killed and then the Rain God would wreak vengeance on the entire Aztec Empire. And what was the likelihood that the Emperor would believe Matzin over his own son, an elite warrior? On the other hand, if Matzin escaped with the girl while everyone was bowing down, Tlaloc would be appeased but he risked angering the Sun God. Out of the corner of his eye he saw his little friend, the salamander scurrying towards him. Then, it struck him! As far as he knew, the law just required being on your

knees and keeping downcast eyes during an eclipse. It didn't say
anything about moving! Quickly and quietly, he crawled towards
the door of the litter and opened it. Lying on the floor with her
eyes closed was the girl. Her feet, hands and mouth were bound.
She was absolutely motionless which worried Matzin until he
remembered that sacrificial victims were always given a potion
to make them sleep so that it would be easier to carry the litter.
He reached in, placed his arms under her body and slid her out.
Then, he draped her over his back with her legs dangling over
his shoulder and began to walk backwards down the pyramid
steps, still on his knees with his eyes downcast.

As he reached the base of the pyramid and started navigating through the sea of prostrate bodies, the moon completely
covered the sun. He crawled through the gates of the temple
precinct and his scraped knees began to leave a trail of blood.
After what seemed like hours, he reached one of the many canals
that crisscrossed the great city. The streets were unusually silent
because everyone was attending the ceremony. Spying a merchant's empty canoe docked on the side of the canal, he crawled
painfully towards it. He gently placed the girl on the bottom of
the vessel, then following her in he grabbed an oar and, still on
his knees, blindly navigated his way towards the lake.

****

Axolo waited impatiently for the sun to reappear so that he
could once and for all take care of this evil brother who had been
haunting his sleep for months. As soon as the eclipse was over,
he would bind the witch's hands, feet and mouth himself and
carry this piece of human garbage to where his father awaited
Tlaloc's female sacrifice.

Axolo was not in the least concerned that the witch who
called himself Matzin would escape during the eclipse. Despite

the fact that the guards had not had time to tie Matzin up, Axolo knew that even witches were subject to the will of the Sun God and would not want to risk angering such a powerful deity by refusing to bow down during an eclipse.

After what seemed like hours, the temple precinct was once again bathed in sunlight. Soon thereafter, the sound of conch shells blowing signaled to the citizens that they could open their eyes and stand up. Axolo quickly leapt to his feet and then gasped in horror at what he saw, or rather didn't see. The witch had vanished, the door to the litter was hanging open, and the victim was nowhere to be seen.

"No!" he screamed, unable to control his rage. The chief knight, who had also quickly assessed the seemingly impossible chain of events, said, "Axolo, act like the warrior that you are! You bring shame to the knights with such an outburst!" Then, turning to the rest of the guards he ordered, "Leave the litter here. There's no need now to carry it through the crowds. Let us proceed directly to the Emperor's vessel. Axolo, you shall be in charge of explaining what has happened here."

How dare he chastise me in front of the other warriors, thought Axolo angrily. He will be sorry he treated me this way when I become Emperor. Then, his heart sank as he thought of his father waiting expectantly at the edge of the lake for Axolo to arrive with Tlaloc's sacrifice. Axolo was furious with Matzin for ruining what should have been a perfect day. Now, instead of receiving praise from his father and the accolades of the crowd, Axolo would be left with the unenviable task of explaining that not only had the Rain God's victim mysteriously disappeared, but Axolo's evil twin had resurfaced and possibly angered the Sun God by performing black magic during an eclipse.

With the chief knight leading the way through the murmuring and frightened crowd, the warriors marched purposefully through the gates of the temple precinct towards the lake.

Just as Matzin was despairing as to whether the sun would ever show its face again, he felt the warm rays on his shoulders and the back of his head. He waited several more minutes to make sure that the golden orb had fully emerged before opening his eyes. The bright glare of the sun on the water nearly blinded him. As he grew accustomed to the daylight, he was overjoyed to see the opposite shore rapidly approaching. The gods surely must have guided this boat today, Matzin thought with amazement, for with my eyes downcast, I had lost all sense of direction and was just praying that I was not going around in circles. He glanced at the beautiful girl lying on the bottom of the boat. She was still under the effects of the sleeping potion she had been given by the Aztec priest. Matzin was once again struck by her beauty. She is finer than jade or the finest quetzal plumes, he marveled.

Everything had happened so fast that he hadn't given any thought to what he would do with the girl once he had rescued her. He decided to bring her home. His parents would know what to do. When he reached the shore, he carefully deposited her on the sand under the shade of the giant maguey plant. Then, he pulled the canoe across the sand and hid it behind a grove of trees, camouflaging it with branches. He hoped this would prevent anyone from discovering where he had escaped to. Returning to where the girl lay, he broke off the tip of one of the maguey plant leaves and squeezed the open end. A yellowy, sticky substance squirted out. He gently rubbed the ointment on the girl's face and arms to ease the pain of sunburn she had received while lying in the boat. Then, he carefully picked her up and, ignoring his own pain and exhaustion, started walking through the forest toward his home.

CHAPTER TWENTY FOUR

When the eclipse of the sun had begun, Ollin was out hunting. His bag already held two fat rabbits but he had really wanted to bring home a plump turkey for dinner. He had seen some wild turkeys in the area a few days ago and had hoped to surprise Ama with one today. But now here he was prostrate on the ground hoping for the Sun God to make the sun soon reappear. Having no choice but to wait, Ollin thought about his wife and how distraught and crazed she had been when she wasn't sure if the snake bite antidote would work. Thankfully, it had worked perfectly and, physically, Matzin was as good as new. His emotional state, however, was another matter. Ollin felt so sorry for his son. Ama had told him about the girl Matzin was infatuated with and the horrible turn of events. Ollin remembered the first time he had seen Ama at a festival in the city. A wreath of red and yellow flowers had lain atop her long silky dark hair. When she had glanced at him with her beautiful brown eyes, he had been immediately smitten. It was inconceivable to imagine the pain Matzin must be feeling knowing that the girl he was falling in love with was being sacrificed today and that he was totally powerless to stop it.

When Ollin had left early this morning to go hunting, he was not surprised to find that Matzin was already awake and had locked himself in the food shed where he was venting his anger by slamming the tlachtli ball against the walls. When Matzin was a young boy and had come home crying because of a cut or bruise, it was easily fixed by one of Ama's many herbs or potions. But, unfortunately, sorcerers had yet to come up with a spell to mend a broken heart.

Ollin's thoughts were suddenly interrupted by the sound of rumbling thunder and then sheets of rain began to fall from the once cloudless sky, drenching Ollin within seconds. Unable to move and seek shelter because of the eclipse, Ollin had no choice but to stay put on the ground which was quickly turning into wet mud. Then, a familiar booming voice could be heard over the storm.

"Ollin, my trusted servant, I come to you with important news. Listen carefully to what I say and meticulously follow my instructions."

There could be no mistake as to who was speaking, Ollin thought. Even without the added effect of the thunderstorm, the voice was that of Tlaloc, the Rain God.

"Tlaloc, my lord, I will of course do whatever you ask of me to the best of my ability," Ollin replied.

"First of all," responded Tlaloc, " I must tell you how proud I am of your adopted son. At great risk to himself, Matzin has single-handedly prevented your fellow countrymen from providing me with an imperfect sacrifice. For that selfless act alone I shall be eternally grateful to him."

Ollin was confused.

"Excuse me, lord, but I don't understand. To what are you referring?"

Tlaloc then recounted how Matzin had confronted the elite warriors, explained to them about the victim's imperfection, been accused of being a witch, and, then, realizing he had no other option, had escaped with the victim while painfully following the letter of the law regarding protocol during an eclipse. Ollin was flabbergasted.

"Where is my son now?" Ollin asked, anxiously, concerned

for his son's safety knowing that the entire Aztec army was most likely searching for him.

"Rest assured no harm has yet come to Matzin. But he is on his way home and it is imperative that you return to your hut quickly. It is time for Matzin to learn the truth about his destiny."

Ollin's heart felt heavy. He had known that one day this moment would come. The young man he and Ama had raised and loved since he was an infant would soon be told a story that would seem unbelievable. It was impossible to know how Matzin would react to the news.

"Listen carefully now to what I am about to say," continued Tlaloc. "Exactly two days after your son returns to the hut, you must accompany Matzin back to the city…"

"But, my lord, the guards will arrest him as soon as we are sighted…" Ollin interrupted in a frightened voice.

"Silence! Am I not the god of rain? What gives you, a mere mortal, the right to even question my plan?" roared Tlaloc as thunder boomed overhead and the rain suddenly turned to hail and pelted Ollin's skin. "Do not dare to interrupt me again!"

"Forgive me, my lord," apologized Ollin.

"After returning to the city, you must go to the palace and demand to see the Emperor. Once within the throne room, you must convincingly reveal the truth to Emperor Toltec about his son, Matzin."

Then, there was a long, stretch of silence such that Ollin felt that he could speak without it being considered an interruption.

"And then, my lord?"

"The future, my dear Ollin, is for the gods to know and for you to only guess at until it is revealed to you at the proper time and place. Is that clear?"

"Yes," Ollin replied.

"Will you remember all of this and do what I

have commanded?"

Every fiber of Ollin's being wanted to scream out, "No! I want to take my wife and son away from the Empire and spare Matzin the grief, pain and danger that I know lies ahead! Find some other man to take on the enormous responsibilities that come with the crown!" But, he knew better than to disobey the gods. So, instead, he nodded his already bowed head and replied quietly, "Yes, Tlaloc."

Immediately after uttering these words, the hail turned into a light rain and then stopped as the sun emerged. Ollin slowly rose to his feet feeling as if he had aged 50 years. Lifting his arrow, quiver and bag of rabbits from the ground, Ollin turned towards home.

****

Ama had been flabbergasted when Matzin had stumbled into the hut carrying an unconscious girl, who turned out to be the girl who had been abducted from the stream. Her son's bloody knees were rubbed raw and he looked exhausted. Earlier in the day, when she had realized that he was no longer playing ball in the shed, she had assumed he was hunting in the nearby forest. If she had known he had gone to the city she would have been a nervous wreck. Sometimes, she thought, it's better that we don't know what our children are up to.

While Matzin told Ama everything that had happened, she prepared a meal for him and placed a poultice on his knees to prevent infection. When he came to the part in the story where the warrior who was next in line to the throne had accused him of being a witch, Ama saw the anger and hurt in her son's eyes. How much more painful it will be for him when Matzin discovers one day that this warrior is also his brother, Ama thought sadly.

Just as Matzin was finishing his account of what had

happened, the girl started to stir. Ama, knowing the girl would be frightened at awakening to strange surroundings, especially after all she had been through, quickly bent down next to her and rubbed her head while repeating in a soothing voice, "You are among friends. You are safe. No one will harm you here."

Pica had been shocked when she opened her eyes and saw a kind, beautiful older woman bending over her. At first, she assumed she must have already been sacrificed and that she was in heaven. But then, out of the corner of her eye, she saw the strange boy who had stared at her every day from the banks of the stream. However, she was too weak to sit up, and the sound of the woman's voice was so comforting, that she just lay there asking questions. The boy, who the older woman called Matzin, filled in the blanks for her. While he spoke, Pica had time to observe him closely for the first time. She realized that he was quite attractive now that he was not performing the strange "swaying dance" that she always saw him do at the stream. She was also impressed that Matzin described what had happened in a very humble manner, although it was obvious that what he had accomplished had been truly spectacular.

When Matzin finished speaking, Pica, with tears running down her cheeks, said, " I and my family shall be forever grateful to you, Matzin, for saving my life. I am sure that as soon as I return home my father will reward you handsomely—for we are not without means."

Matzin blushed and mumbled in reply, "That will be completely unnecessary. By sparing your life, I have prevented my people from bearing the brunt of Tlaloc's wrath. That is reward enough for me."

Ama smiled, pleased with her son's response.

"It's funny," Pica said, turning to Ama, "When I was a young girl the other children used to tease me because of my birthmark. I grew to hate this purple stain so much that I would rub the bottom of my foot with rocks until it was raw and bleeding, hoping to remove it. My mother would rock me in her arms and tell me that when people made fun of something that was different it just exposed their own ignorance. She told me that I was lucky to have such a mark because it meant the gods had singled me out for great things. At the time, I thought she was just making up a story to make me feel better, but today that birthmark saved my life, so maybe there is some truth to what she said after all."

"I am sure your mother was right," replied Ama. "My son was also born with a birthmark."

"Really? Where?" asked Pica.

"Here," replied Matzin as he removed his cloak and held up his arm.

Pica's face immediately turned pale. Matzin quickly lowered his arm, angry and hurt that she seemed disgusted by his large purple birthmark even though she had one herself. He turned to leave but stopped as she cried out, "Matzin, please don't leave! You misunderstand my reaction. I'm only shocked because your birthmark seems to be the exact same shape as mine. Look." She pulled her blanket off and Ama and Matzin saw that Pica was not mistaken.

"Well, I guess that means I'm destined for great things too," Matzin joked.

Oh, if you only knew, thought Ama. If you only knew. Just then, Ollin entered the hut and laid down his bag of fresh kill. Pica screamed and Ama rushed to reassure her.

"Pica, this is my husband, Ollin. He will not hurt you."

Looking back towards the entrance to the hut, Ama immediately noticed that something was bothering Ollin by the pained expression on his face. She also observed that Ollin didn't seem surprised to see a strange girl lying on a mat in the middle of their home.

"What's wrong, my love?" Ama asked.

Ollin walked to his wife, embraced her and whispered in her ear, "I had a visit from Tlaloc today. Come outside. We need to talk."

"Matzin," Ama said to her son. " I need to help your father with something. Stay with Pica and see if you can get her to eat something."

Matzin was only too happy to oblige. He brought a steaming bowl of broth over to Pica and helped lift her into a sitting position so that she could drink it. Then, they started to talk as if they had known each other for years. It was as if knowing that they shared a similar birthmark had suddenly made them fast friends. She told him about her village and her family. It was obvious that she missed them and couldn't wait to get home.

"They must be extremely worried about me," she said.

"As soon as you are healthy enough to travel, I'll take you home myself," Matzin responded, although he wished he could keep her here forever. It was great to have someone his own age to talk to.

Tez, however, was disgusted with Matzin. Why had the boy brought the girl with him? Now, the entire Aztec army would be looking for them. What could one small salamander, albeit a crafty one, and one young man do against hundreds of well-trained warriors? Matzin seemed to enjoy placing himself in danger. And now here he was smiling and laughing with the girl who had caused this whole mess. Unbelievable. He walked outside to get some fresh air and overheard Ollin and Ama talking near the food shed.

"...So, the time has finally come," Ama sighed. "When you and Matzin leave for the city, I will keep Pica here with me until her strength returns. Then, I will bring her back to her village." Tez stopped dead in his tracks. Keep the girl here? Was everyone in this family crazy? The Aztec warriors would not react kindly when they found out Matzin's parents were sheltering the Rain God's intended victim. The little salamander scurried into his little hole and tried to come up with a plan to force the girl to leave. But the stress of the escape and the warmth of the hole made Tez tired and soon he was fast asleep.

CHAPTER TWENTY FIVE

Emperor Toltec was sitting on his throne deep in thought. The past twenty-four hours had been horrific and he feared that things were going to get worse before they got better. Looking back, it was the eclipse that seemed to have been the catalyst for the string of bad luck that had since followed.

Shortly after the conch shells had blown signaling the end of the eclipse, he had seen a group of warriors approaching the lake. He was puzzled and concerned when he realized that they were not carrying a litter. When they finally arrived at his vessel and his son, Axolo, explained that the evil twin had spirited away the sacrificial victim flaunting the Sun God, Toltec had been stunned. Was the son who had been raised by witches trying to purposefully destroy the Empire and possibly the entire world by incurring the Sun God's wrath? Was he seeking revenge against a father who had abandoned him? It was a frightening thought.

Toltec had immediately ordered Axolo to quickly find another victim before sundown to avoid adding the Rain God's anger to the other misfortunes. Fortunately, Axolo had success-fully completed this task and the new victim had been drowned mere moments before the sun had sunk below the volcanic mountains that rimmed the lake.

However, Toltec did not attend the subdued celebration which followed the sacrifice. Shortly after Axolo had left to find another victim, one of the palace guards had come running up to tell Toltec that his wife, Mia, had fainted at the beginning of the eclipse and was still unconscious. Toltec had hurried back to the palace where Etta, Mia's trusted servant and friend, had met him at the door to Mia's chambers. He had known immediately by the look on her face that the news was not good.

"What has happened, Etta?" he had demanded.

"Sire, our beloved Mia has lapsed into a coma."

"What? How can this be?" he had cried out in agony.

"The difficult childbirth she endured years ago must have weakened Mia's heart. I believe that she became frightened at the start of the eclipse and her body was not strong enough to cope with the anxiety."

"But she will recover, right?" he had asked, hopefully.

"I don't know, Sire. With your permission, I would like to send for Ollin the sorcerer. He is one of the best healers in the Empire. If anyone can do something for the Empress, it is him."

"I am familiar with Ollin's great powers. I shall send our swiftest warrior to bring Ollin back to the palace at once."

Now, Toltec was left with nothing to do but wait. Trying to keep his mind off the thought of losing his precious Mia, he had tried to see Kan, the high priest, to discuss the reappearance of his abandoned evil son. But Kan was still delirious from his illness and the other priests, fearing Kan would infect the Emperor, would not let Toltec even enter the calmecac building. So he sat alone in the throne room, while his subjects enjoyed the sumptuous feast that had been prepared for Tlaloc's spring ceremony, unaware that they might soon mourn the death of their queen.

CHAPTER TWENTY SIX

Tez was worried. Ollin and Matzin had locked themselves in the food shed just after the evening meal, hours ago, and had yet to reappear. Inside the hut, the girl was sleeping but Ama was sitting quietly staring at the dying embers in the hearth and periodically wiping tears from her eyes. What in the heavens' name is going on? Tez wondered.

Just then the shed door opened and as the two men came out, Tez was alarmed to see that Matzin was very pale and Ollin looked exhausted. Placing his arm on his son's shoulder, Ollin said, "I know this news has come as a tremendous shock to you." Turning towards his father and taking hold of both of his hands, Matzin replied, "Despite what you have just revealed to me, I shall always think of you and Ama as my true parents." Moved, Ollin answered, "And you shall always be our son, Matzin. And it's not as if your mother and I are going anywhere. We will be here for you whenever you need us and we will expect frequent visits."

"What time must we leave for the city?"

"I think we should leave at daybreak. For now, let's try to sleep, for you'll need your strength and wits about you tomorrow."

Matzin nodded to placate his father, but knew it would be impossible to fall asleep after all that he had just learned. It was frightening, exciting and overwhelming all at the same time. He couldn't help thinking that Pica would be impressed when she found out that her rescuer was in line to be the next Aztec Emperor.

Matzin knows, thought the little salamander. He scurried over to where the boy was lying down and scrambled inside his leather pouch. Tez had no intention of being left behind tomorrow.

****

A warrior came running towards Ollin and Matzin as they approached the city on the southern causeway. Because it was so early, the walkway was empty except for a few farmers and merchants walking to town. Matzin, his head bowed, draped in a drab brown cloak, walked closely behind Ollin, hoping that no one would recognize him from the day of the eclipse and thereby prevent him from getting to the palace.

"Halt, gentlemen!" cried the soldier as he came within arm's reach of the two travelers. Ollin turned to Matzin and whispered, "Stay where you are and let me do the talking." Then, turning back towards the warrior, he was startled to see the soldier kneeling before him.

"Ollin, sir," said the warrior deferentially, "You may not remember me, but my name is Colco. You healed my mother and saved her from certain death."

"Of course I remember you, Colco. I trust your mother is still doing well?"

"Yes, sir. Better than ever."

"That's wonderful. But surely that is not why you have stopped me in the middle of the causeway."

"No, sir. The Emperor has sent me to look for you. His wife, Empress Mia, has fallen into a coma and he hopes you can help her."

"By all means, Colco. How awful! My assistant and I will follow you to the palace at once."

Colco glanced at the hooded assistant who was quite tall for an Aztec man. Although Ollin was distressed to hear about the queen, he couldn't help but be relieved that he and Matzin had unexpectedly been provided with an armed escort to take them immediately to the palace.

As the causeway ended and they entered the city streets, it became more congested. Matzin found it harder and harder to stay close to Ollin as they weaved in and out of the crowds. Suddenly, an old woman stumbled in front of Matzin and her basket, which was filled to the brim with clean laundry, fell out of her hands onto the ground. Instinctively, Matzin bent down to pick it up for her.

"Are you all right?" he asked solicitously as he handed her the basket, which luckily had landed upright.

"Yes, I'm fine, young man. Just a little shaken up. Thank you for your help. I must have tripped over something. My eyes aren't what they used to be."

As she turned to go he realized that a clean, white tunic from her basket had fallen on the ground. He grabbed it and lifted it up yelling, "Excuse me, ma'am. You left this cloak behind."

****

Axolo was watching a game of patolli. He had finished his morning chores early, including leaving some dead mice for his owl, who was sleeping peacefully. He was trying to keep his mind off his mother and her precarious health. Ever since that evil witch had reappeared, nothing seemed to be going right. Just then, the hairs on Axolo's neck stood up as he heard the unmistakable voice of Matzin, the witch. He turned and couldn't believe his eyes. Matzin was standing in the middle of the street holding up a white garment and yelling something unintelligible. Probably some sort of curse, thought Axolo. Even if Axolo hadn't recognized his evil brother's face, the fearsome-looking birthmark on Matzin's upraised arm was undeniable.

"You will not escape from me this time," Axolo vowed to himself as he removed his cloak and stealthily moved towards the witch, hoping to catch him from behind.

****

Ollin was not surprised to see Emperor Toltec in the distance waiting anxiously at the palace gates. The sorcerer knew how much Toltec loved his wife and how horrible it must feel to be the most powerful man in the Empire and yet powerless to help Empress Mia. He turned to see how Matzin was holding up and then gasped. Matzin was nowhere to be seen.

"Stop, Colco," he cried out to the young warrior ahead of him. "I've lost my assistant."

"I'm sorry, Ollin, but we need to keep moving. I'm under strict orders to deliver you to the palace as quickly as possible. No detours."

"I understand, Colco," Ollin replied, frantically scanning the crowd behind them as they climbed the palace steps. Where was his son? His thoughts were interrupted by Toltec's commanding voice.

"Ollin, at last! Follow me to the Empress' chambers. Colco, you are dismissed."

Ollin quickly turned to Colco and whispered urgently, "Colco, please go back and find my assistant and escort him to the palace. There's no time to explain why, but he might be in grave danger."

Colco, happy to perform a favor for the man who had saved his mother's life, sprinted back in the direction from which they had just come.

****

Before Matzin knew what was happening, someone pulled something over his upper body and held it fast around him such that Matzin's arms were pinned against his sides. It was wrapped so tightly around his face that he was having trouble breathing. He tried to struggle free but whoever it was that was holding him captive was incredibly strong. Matzin started to panic as he realized this person was trying to kill him. He made one last effort to break free and then, unable to breathe, he became incredibly dizzy. The last thing he heard before he lost consciousness was a familiar voice saying, "Now you will never take what is rightfully mine."

****

Colco spotted Ollin's assistant inexplicably holding up a white tunic in the middle of the street. Luckily, he was easy to recognize because he was several inches taller than everyone else in the crowd. As Colco started to run towards the assistant, he saw what looked like Axolo creeping up behind the tall, young man. Incredulously, Colco watched as Axolo threw a cloak over the assistant's head. Colco had never forgiven Axolo for tricking him out of winning the tree-climbing ceremony by lying to him about his mother's health. And now that lying, cheating no-good warrior was hurting a sorcerer's assistant. Unbelievable. Without thinking of the punishment he could receive for intentionally harming an elite warrior, Colco rushed through the crowd and slammed into Axolo, knocking him and his captive to the ground. Axolo leapt up, enraged, to find Colco standing defiantly in front of him.

"How dare you attack a member of the elite corps? I'll see you banished from the Empire for this!" Axolo yelled.

171

"You call yourself a warrior?" Colco replied sarcastically, "What kind of warrior harms an unarmed Aztec citizen for no reason? It is you who shall be punished, Axolo, not I."

"For no reason, you imbecile? Do you know who this is?" Axolo responded, pointing to Matzin's inert body laying on the ground and still covered by Axolo's cloak.

"Actually, I do," replied Colco. "It is Ollin the sorcerer's trusted assistant. He and Ollin have come to the city to try to heal your mother, the Empress. I can assure you that neither Ollin nor your father will be pleased to see how you have treated him."

"On the contrary, I think they will be very pleased. This piece of filth is none other than the witch who angered our gods by stealing the sacrificial victim on the day of the eclipse."

Upon hearing this news, the crowd gasped in horror and moved quickly away from the young man lying motionless in the dirt. Colco was momentarily nonplussed. Could he have made a terrible mistake? If Axolo was right, Colco would be severely punished. There was only one thing left to do.

"Let's take him to the palace and let the Emperor decide which one of us is right."

"Fine with me, Colco."

Tez scrambled out of the pouch and under the cloak that covered Matzin's upper torso. He was relieved to feel the boy's heart still beating, although weakly. He moved his way toward Matzin's face and realized that the cloak was pushed against the boy's nose, cutting off his air supply. With as much strength as he could muster, the salamander arched his back creating an air space, so that Matzin could begin to breathe again. Tez prayed that someone would remove this cloak soon, for he wasn't sure how much longer he would be able to remain in this uncomfortable position.

Axolo reached down, picked up Matzin, roughly slung him over his shoulder and started walking confidently toward the palace. Colco followed, hoping that this was not his last day in the kingdom.

CHAPTER TWENTY SEVEN

Ollin took out several different colored rocks from his leather pouch, ground them into a fine powder and placed the powder in a ceramic mug. After adding water, he instructed Etta to gently hold Mia's mouth open. Then, he rubbed the paste-like substance on the Empress' tongue while murmuring an incantation. After completing this ritual he said, "Now, we must just be patient and wait. If the potion is effective, we should see some improvement by tomorrow."

"Is there nothing else I can do to help her get better?" asked Etta, feeling unusually helpless.

"Massage her feet and hands to keep her circulation going and turn her from side to side several times per hour so that she does not get bedsores. It is also important that she remain hydrated. Pour several drops of water down her throat every five minutes or so."

Just then, one of the palace guards appeared at the doorway.

"Excuse me, Sire. I'm sorry to interrupt you but your son, Axolo, is waiting for you in the throne room. He says he has urgent business to discuss. He entered the palace with an inert body of a man draped over his shoulder and was accompanied by another warrior. But, when questioned, refused to discuss the situation with anyone but you."

Toltec, who was kneeling next to his wife and holding her hand, turned to Ollin and asked, "Are you done here?"

"Yes, Sire," said Ollin, worried that the motionless body that the guard had mentioned was that of his son.

"Then, why don't you accompany me back to the throne room. I will have my servants prepare something for you to eat and drink."

Planting a kiss on his wife's pale forehead, Toltec exited the room at a brisk pace with Ollin following closely behind.

While waiting for his father to arrive, Axolo took advantage of Matzin's unconscious state. He first removed the cloak and was startled to see a salamander leap off the boy's face and scurry away. He then bound Matzin's feet, hands and mouth so that if Matzin regained consciousness he would be unable to perform any of his black magic.

With each passing moment Colco, who was standing at attention in the corner of the room, grew more unsure as to whether he or Axolo was right about the identity of the boy. But there was no turning back now.

Just then, Toltec strode into the room followed by Ollin. Axolo was startled to see the sorcerer who had saved his owl. Then, he remembered Ollin had come to help his mother. Seeing his son tied up and lying motionless on the ground, Ollin turned towards Colco and cried out, "What happened?"

Before Colco could reply, Axolo, ignoring Ollin's outburst, approached his father and bowed down saying, "Father, I have captured the witch who abducted Tlaloc's sacrificial victim."

"How can you be certain that this is he, Axolo?" replied Toltec.

Axolo turned the boy onto his stomach and pointed to the birthmark on one of the boy's arms that were tied behind his back. It was the Emperor's turn to gasp in amazement. He walked over to the boy and gently turned him onto his back again. There was no mistake. This was his abandoned son. Even if there had been no visible birthmark, Toltec would have known. The boy looked like a masculine version of Mia. His beloved Mia. For the first time, he was thankful that his wife was in a coma because the shock of coming face to face with a son that she didn't even know existed would have certainly killed her. He had to admit that the thought of the severe punishment, although deserved, that awaited this young boy, who had been unfortunate enough to be cursed with an unlucky destiny, was making him feel ill.

Then the room seemed to be spinning. Ollin, realizing that Toltec was close to fainting from shock, guided the Emperor to his throne. Then, pulling a purple-colored herb from his pouch, he crumbled it in his fist and held his hand up to Toltec's nose. The pungent, bitter smell allowed Toltec to regain his senses.

Axolo stared intently at his father waiting expectantly for some praise. But Toltec just sat there silently staring at Matzin. Finally, Axolo could stand it no longer.

"Father, are you not pleased?"

"Of course, Axolo," replied the Emperor in a voice that lacked conviction. "It was very courageous of you to attempt such a capture. You shall be generously rewarded for your bravery."

Bravery, thought the salamander disdainfully from the corner of the throne room. To attack an unarmed man from behind?

Thank you, Sire," replied Axolo. "And may I also recommend that Colco, the warrior who accompanied me here, be severely punished for insubordination."

Toltec could not hide his surprise at this accusation. The priests and other warriors always spoke highly of Colco. In fact, one priest had told the Emperor that Colco was the most trustworthy of all the calmecac students.

"What did Colco do that would warrant such a serious charge?" Toltec asked his son.

"Shortly after I had captured the witch, Colco intentionally knocked me to the ground. Fortunately, the witch was already unconscious or the consequences could have been disastrous."

Puzzled, the Emperor turned to Colco, "Is this true, Colco?"

"Yes, Sire. But please let me explain."

"Continue."

"When I came upon Ollin this morning, he was accompanied by an assistant. But as we wended our way through the crowds, we somehow became separated from the assistant. Not wanting to delay our arrival at the palace, I brought Ollin directly here. Then, I promised Ollin that I would retrace our route and look for this assistant who Ollin warned me might be in danger..."

"Is this true, Ollin?" interrupted Toltec.

"Yes, Sire," replied Ollin.

"Go on, Colco."

"Finally, spotting the young man up ahead, I started to run towards him when I saw Axolo attack him from behind and place a cloak over his upper body. A struggle ensued. Believing I was protecting Ollin's assistant from danger, I charged at Axolo knocking him over."

"Colco, I must admit that for the first time I am disappointed in you. Your first duty is to your fellow warriors. If you had any question as to the reasons behind Axolo's actions you should have confronted him face to face. But, to knock him down and shame him publicly is inexcusable. If the witch had gotten free because of your actions, who knows what might have happened?"

"I deeply regret disappointing you, Sire. But, in my defense, I must say that the young man lying here on the floor looks remarkably like Ollin's assistant. And if I had waited to confront Axolo face to face, the young man might have died from asphyxiation."

"Regardless of what you thought, Colco, Axolo has earned the right to be your superior and, therefore, you were required to defer to his judgment. Is that clear?"

"Yes, Sire," Colco replied, wishing he could wipe the smug,

gloating look off Axolo's face with his fist.

Turning to Ollin, Toltec said, "Ollin, I had no idea that you had brought an assistant with you and that you are concerned for his safety. Before I determine appropriate punishments for Colco and the witch, let me send one of my guards with you to find your trusted assistant."

"Thank you, Sire," replied Ollin. "But that will not be necessary. Colco's instincts were correct. My assistant is lying on the ground before you."

Take that, you mean old thug! thought Tez as he glared at Axolo from his shadowed corner.

"What are you talking about, Ollin?" exclaimed Toltec in disbelief.

"The gods have decreed that it is time you learned the truth about your son," replied Ollin softly.

"You mean Axolo?" asked Toltec, confused.

"No, Sire. Your fifth son. Matzin."

CHAPTER TWENTY EIGHT

As Ollin began to recount how he had found the infant by the large maguey plant and had been directed by the gods to raise the baby as his own son, Axolo's face grew increasingly more pale.

"Ollin," interrupted the Emperor, weary and confused, "Why would the gods instruct you to care for a boy who was destined to be raised by witches?"

Now it was Ollin's turn to be confused. "Sire, what are you talking about?" Toltec sadly explained the circumstances of Matzin's birth and the evil sign under which he was born.

"Ollin," said the Emperor, fighting back tears as he relived painful memories, "it broke my heart to abandon my son to the witches, but after the high priest revealed his destiny, I had no choice."

"Sire," Ollin replied, "According to the Rain God, this boy, whose name is Matzin, is to be the successor to the throne. That is his true destiny."

Toltec shook his head violently and exclaimed, "I refuse to believe that the gods are so displeased with our people that they would desire a man born under such an evil sign to rule over and most likely destroy the Aztec Empire. We need guidance in this matter."

Turning to one of his guards, the Emperor asked, "Is it true that Kan's health has improved such that he is now coherent?"

"Yes, Sire," replied the guard.

"Then, bring him to the palace. Tell him that I must speak with him immediately!."

Before the guard could respond, Axolo quickly spoke up.

"Father, why don't you let me go? The high priest may still be too weak to walk on his own. I am strong enough to carry him here."

"Very well, Axolo. Go quickly."

As Axolo exited the throne room, Ollin asked for and received permission to approach Matzin, who was starting to stir. Ollin was relieved to find that his son's pulse was normal. He surreptitiously extracted a powdery substance from his pouch and placed it inside Matzin's nose. This would cause Matzin to sleep peacefully for a few more hours. Hopefully by then everything would be resolved in Matzin's favor and his son would no longer have to be tied up like an animal.

Toltec sadly watched the sorcerer lovingly stroke Matzin's head. He had known Ollin for as long as he could remember and had always trusted the sorcerer's judgment. But he hoped that in this case, Ollin had misunderstood the gods' instructions. If a witch were truly destined to be the successor to the throne, the Aztec Empire was in great danger.

****

When Axolo entered the calmecac building, he overheard the priests talking.

"Well, Kan seems a little stronger today."

"But, he still needs to rest and not be bothered."

"Yes, the doctors have said that the slightest anxiety could cause a relapse."

Music to my ears, thought Axolo. He turned left and walked down an empty hall that led directly to Kan's chambers. Axolo was pleased to find that the high priest was alone.

Kan, who had been resting, opened his eyes when he heard someone enter the room. He was surprised to see Axolo standing there.

'Hello, Axolo," Kan said feebly, "Is there something I can help you with or is this purely a social call?"

"I, of course, am pleased to see that you are feeling better, sir," Axolo replied insincerely, "But I have been sent here by my father. The Emperor wants you to come directly to the palace. He has an urgent matter to discuss with you regarding a witch who was recently captured. If you are too weak to travel, I will assist you."

"A witch?" Kan exclaimed, trembling as visions of his horrific childhood encounter with witches flashed through his mind.

"Yes," replied Axolo, "In fact, you are very familiar with this particular witch. He is easily recognizable due to the hideous purple birthmark on his arm."

Kan's already pale face turned another shade whiter and his eye began to twitch. Now, different recollections flooded his brain. As if it were yesterday, he remembered how frightened he had been carrying the newborn baby toward the witches' enclave. Then, his horror as he realized his mistake and returned to find the infant already gone! The tormenting memory of that mistake would haunt him for the rest of his life.

"Why does the Emperor need me?" Kan stammered. "The law is very clear and needs no interpretation by me. If a witch enters the capital city, he or she shall be put to death."

"Well," responded Axolo, "There is a slight complication. Ollin, the sorcerer claims he found this witch as a newborn babe, and raised him as his own. According to Ollin, this Matzin, as he calls him, is not a witch at all, but is instead destined to take Toltec's place on the throne."

Kan gasped with incredulity as he thought of the ramifications of this revelation. Axolo continued, "Understandably, the

Emperor is confused. Even if Ollin is telling the truth, this does not change the fact that you revealed long ago that this Matzin was born under the most evil sign imaginable. And, of course, you would never have made a mistake regarding something so vital to the future of the Aztec nation. Would you?"

Kan could not respond. His tongue suddenly felt as swollen as a pregnant woman's belly and his mouth was very dry. His face became flushed and his pulse started to race. Yes, he, the great honorable high priest, had made such a mistake. His head felt as if someone was driving a machete through it. How could he stand before the Emperor now, after so many years, and reveal the truth of Matzin's true birth sign and how he had so horribly botched his assignment? It was inconceivable. Slowly, his thoughts turned to how wonderful it had been while he was so sick to be in a dreamlike state where all of his fears and regrets were forgotten. It would be so nice to be there now. The high priest gratefully felt himself slip away from the horrific reality that surrounded him.

Axolo watched exulatantly as Kan's eyes closed and his breathing became shallow. Axolo waited to be sure that Kan was no longer conscious, then rushed out of the room and ran up to Teo, the priest that had been taking over Kan's duties during his convalescence.

"Come quickly, sir!" Axolo cried, "Kan has taken a turn for the worse!"

"What?" exclaimed the priest as he ran down the hall. "I just saw spoke with him moments ago. What happened and what were you doing in the high priest's chambers?"

"I had been sent by the Emperor who had a matter of great importance to discuss with him. I was supposed to bring him back to the palace but when I entered his room, he suddenly became feverish and lost consciousness."

They arrived at Kan's room and Teo immediately confirmed

that the high priest had indeed slipped back into a coma.

"I don't understand…" murmured the priest.

"I'm sorry this has happened," said Axolo, "But right now I am responsible for bringing the high priest to the throne room for an urgent consultation with the Emperor. I do not want to return empty-handed. Since he is clearly unavailable, you must come in his place."

"Of course," replied the priest, in a dazed voice, still bewildered by the unexpected change in Kan's condition.

****

Toltec was surprised and concerned when Axolo returned accompanied by Teo instead of the high priest.

"Where is Kan?" he asked. Teo explained how the high priest had inexplicably lost consciousness again but that they were all hoping for the best.

"May I may be of service to you in his place, Sire?" added the priest.

Toltec dearly wished Kan were there instead, because the high priest was intimately familiar with the history of what had happened so many years ago. The Emperor had hoped Kan would shed some light on how best to proceed. But wishful thinking was like washing a brand new cloak… a complete waste of time. So, he began to tell Teo the story of the birth of his twin sons and the divergent paths they were destined to follow based on Kan's reading of their respective birth signs. The Emperor finished by adding, "The story has now become even more complicated because Ollin has just revealed that he has raised the evil twin from birth. The gods have apparently told him that Matzin, not Axolo, should succeed to the throne."

Over my dead body, thought Axolo, as he ground his teeth together and clenched his fists.

"I can only hope that there has been some mistake or miscommunication," Toltec admitted, "If not, are the gods so displeased with my leadership that they would choose someone born under such an unfavorable sign, possibly a witch, to be the next Emperor?"

If Matzin is a witch, thought Tez disgustedly from his vantage point in the corner of the room, then I'm a hummingbird. How he wished the gods would grant him the power of speech for just one minute!

Teo felt sick to his stomach. He had proudly dedicated his life to learning and upholding the laws of this great people. But now, these same laws prevented him from telling the Emperor the truth. If he could reveal the devastating information he had learned from Kan during the high priest's confession, this matter could be cleared up immediately. However, the law was clear. A priest who heard a confession was bound by secrecy as long as the confessor was still alive. The punishment for breaking this vow was death by drowning. Teo understood the policy behind such a harsh rule. If the citizens feared that their confessions might become public, they would be unwilling to confess and, therefore, would go to the afterlife burdened by their sins. How unfortunate that Kan had become unconscious just when they sorely needed his testimony the most. There was only one thing left to do.

"Sire, we only have one option in this rather unusual case," said Teo finally.

"Go on," replied Toltec.

"In situations like these where there are conflicting predictions of future events and the Emperor needs to resolve the conflict in order to properly guide our people, the law is clear. A ball game shall be used as a form of divination. Each player shall be assigned a certain outcome. Therefore, Axolo and Matzin shall play a match. If Axolo wins, he shall be the rightful successor to the throne and Matzin shall be deemed a witch and banished. If, on the other hand, Matzin is the victor, Matzin shall be the next Aztec Emperor despite his birthsign."

"But what if Matzin uses witchcraft to win the game?" Toltec asked.

"Sire," Ollin interrupted, losing his temper, "Matzin may have been born under an unfavorable sign, which I do not believe, but he has never been exposed to the evils of witchcraft!"

"And even if he is a witch," added Teo, "It would be obvious to any spectator at the game if he were about to cast a spell, at which time Matzin would be forcibly restrained by the guards and Axolo would be deemed the winner."

Satisfied, Toltec said, "All right. Let's get this over with as soon as possible. The game will be tomorrow afternoon. Meanwhile, just to be on the safe side, Matzin will be placed in a windowless room in the palace and heavily guarded."

"Sire, may I stay with him?" Ollin asked. "Someone will need to explain to him what has happened when he wakes up."

"As you wish, Ollin," the Emperor replied, "And we will provide him with the equipment he needs for tomorrow's game. Guards, carry Matzin to his room and stand watch outside the door."

Ollin followed the soldiers out of the throne room. As they passed Axolo, Ollin saw the warrior stare at Matzin with unveiled hatred. Comparing his tall, lean son with this brawny, muscular warrior, Ollin feared not only that Matzin would lose tomorrow, but that he would be killed in the process.

Axolo almost laughed out loud. He couldn't have asked for a better solution. He was sure he would easily win tomorrow's match. He was, after all, the undefeated champion. Then, his scrawny interfering brother would be banished for life and Axolo would become the next Emperor.

"May I be excused, Father? I would like to prepare for

tomorrow's important game."

"Yes, son," replied Toltec distractedly.

As Axolo strode confidently out the door, Tez scurried after Ollin. This was just horrible! he thought. How could they allow the fate of the Aztec people to rest on the outcome of a silly, little game? It was insane! He was at a loss as to how he would help Matzin get out of this one.

The Emperor was left alone with his thoughts. He did not relish watching his two sons compete tomorrow. Matzin was clearly outmatched. And, what if, as Ollin had implied, Kan had been wrong about the birth signs? No…he couldn't think that way or he would drive himself crazy. Until Kan could speak for himself, it was not worth agonizing over. Let the gods decide the outcome tomorrow. It was out of his hands now. He slowly stood and walked towards his wife's chambers to see if she were feeling better.

CHAPTER TWENTY NINE

The moon shone through the window as Omo the owl woke from a deep sleep. Axolo was meticulously laying out his protective gear: knee caps, leather apron and gloves, chin piece and half-mask. There must be a ball game tomorrow, Omo said happily to herself. The owl knew that Axolo had won every match he had ever played. She could sleep peacefully tomorrow confident that the young warrior would not need her help.

****

Ama woke early after a restless sleep. She was worried about her son. She couldn't help wondering how the Emperor had reacted to the news about Matzin – assuming that her husband and son had even made it safely to the palace. She glanced over at Pica sleeping on the mat next to her. Ama had grown quite fond of the young girl. She was well-mannered and kind. As a thank you for caring for her, Pica had cooked an excellent meal for the two of them last night and their lively conversation had kept Ama from dwelling on her son's fate. But now, in the silent cold of the early morning light, she had nothing to distract her from her anxious thoughts. Maybe if she kept busy it would help.

"Pica," she whispered next to Pica's ear.

Pica slowly opened her eyes. "Yes, Ama?"

"I'm sorry to wake you but I didn't want you to worry if you woke up and I was gone."

"What? Where are you going?"

"Just down to the shore. There is a large maguey plant there and I need the juice from its leaves for a healing ointment that I make."

"I will go with you then," Pica replied as she started to stand.

"Thank you Pica, I would love the company. But do you feel strong enough?"

"I feel completely better today, Ama, thanks to you. In fact, I was wondering if when Ollin and Matzin return from the city one of you could take me back to my village. I miss my family and I'm sure they are worried sick about me."

Pica had only been told that Matzin and Ollin had to go to the city on business and that they weren't sure how long they would be gone.

"Let me observe you this morning on our walk to the lake, and if it seems like you will be able to handle the uphill journey, I'll take you home myself after our morning meal."

"Thank you Ama! You have been so kind to me."

They left the hut together and walked down the dirt path towards the lake. As they approached the shore, Ama saw two canoes on the sand. Two men stood knee-deep in the lake, fishing. By the number of fish already piled in their boats, Ama guessed the fishermen had been there for hours and would soon be returning to the city to sell their catches of the day.

Turning to Pica, Ama said, "Why don't you wait for me here? If either of those men recognizes you as the sacrificial victim that was stolen away, we could be in real trouble. I'll go down and get what I need from the maguey plant and then we'll go back to the hut."

"You read my mind, Ama," said Pica gratefully as she

stepped back and hid behind a large tree.

As Ama got closer to the large spiny plant she heard the fishermen's conversation.

"….The last time I remember a ball game being used to predict the future was when I was just a little boy. And the stadium was packed. We'll be lucky if we get in at all."

"My brother knows one of the guards at the entrance and he says he'll be able to save a place for me."

"The Sun God must be shining down upon you."

"Care to bet on the outcome?"

"Only if I get to pick Axolo as the winner. He's the best ball player I've ever seen and he has yet to lose a match."

"It is true that he glitters like a precious stone. However, because this is a game of divination, the gods will have a hand in the outcome."

"True. But I refuse to believe that the gods would allow the witch who stole the Rain God's sacrifice to triumph over the Emperor's own son.'

"Did you hear that the revered sorcerer, Ollin, claims that Axolo's opponent is not a witch at all but instead was raised by him and his wife?"

"Yes. I also heard that the witch is actually the Emperor's son. And if both of those stories are true, I'm of noble birth with a jade nose plug."

The other fisherman laughed.

"Well, we should get back to the city so we can sell some of this fish before the game starts."

As they paddled away in their canoes, Ama, who had been paralyzed by what she had heard, rushed to where Pica was hiding.

"Pica, I know I promised that I would take you home today but I must go to the city instead."

The young girl had never seen Ama so distressed and agitated.

"What's wrong, Ama? Is it Matzin and Ollin? What did the fishermen say that has upset you so?"

"I'm sorry but I have no time to explain right now. Will you be all right by yourself while I'm gone?"

"What are you talking about? I'm going with you," Pica exclaimed.

"Don't be ridiculous," replied Ama in an exasperated tone, "If you are recognized you could be in great danger."

"I could wear one of your hooded cloaks. No one would notice me. Please, Ama. I don't want to stay here by myself."

Not wanting to waste time arguing, Ama said, "All right. Race back to the hut and grab one of my cloaks."

Pica ran off before Ama could change her mind.

****

With a determined look on his face, Matzin attached the wide leather belt around his hips, which hopefully would blunt the impact of a hard-driven ball. Ollin stood quietly in the corner of the room watching his son. He understood that Matzin needed to focus all of his energy on the upcoming game. It was no time for small talk.

When Matzin had awoken from his drug-induced slumber, Ollin had explained that a ball game would determine the rightful heir to the throne. The sorcerer purposefully did not tell him about supposedly being born under an evil sign. First of all, Ollin refused to believe it. Second, it would only cause Matzin unnecessary worry. His son couldn't afford to have any other distractions today.

Matzin's head was filled with conflicting emotions. On the one hand, he still hadn't quite digested the fact that he had supposedly been chosen by the gods to be the next Emperor of the Aztec people. He, of course, felt incredibly honored and excited; who wouldn't be? But it was scary to think that the fate of the Empire might rest in his hands. Also, he had seen Axolo play. How could he possibly beat a champion when his only opponent had been a food shed wall?

Matzin was startled out of his thoughts by a knock on the door. A guard entered and declared, "We will escort you to the stadium in 10 minutes. Do you have everything you require?"

"Yes, thank you," replied Matzin, "I will be ready."

The guard left, securing the door behind him. Matzin still had trouble believing that the outcome of this ball game against Axolo would determine his destiny. Visions of the cocky warrior flashed through his brain: Axolo decisively victorious and cruel in the only ball game Matzin had ever seen; Axolo abducting the girl Matzin had fallen in love with; Axolo falsely accusing him of being a witch on the temple steps; and Axolo attacking him from behind in the marketplace. The bile in his throat started to rise. He would give anything to be the one who finally defeated Axolo on the ball court. He strapped on his knee caps, his half mask and his chin piece. Finally, he picked up his leather gloves.

"Are you ready, son?" Ollin asked, finally breaking the silence.

"As ready as I'll ever be," responded Matzin.

Placing his hands on Matzin's shoulders, Ollin said, "Before you go, I just want you to know how proud your mother and I are of you. You have grown up to be a fine young man, worthy of leading your people. You don't need me to tell you that this will be a difficult match today but I feel you are up to the task. It is important that you stay focused. Axolo is an angry, bitter young man. He will probably try to taunt you, to distract you. Just imagine that his slurs are insignificant little flies and brush them from your body. Finally, remember that you have one thing Axolo doesn't: a revelation from the gods that you are the chosen one. I will be praying for you."

"Thank you, Father," Matzin replied. Then, as much as he didn't want to think about it, it struck him that he could be killed today. It was important that he say something before the guards returned.

"Father, I want you to know that you and Ama will always be my true parents. I have no hard feelings toward Toltec; in fact, I would have done the same thing in his place under similar circumstances. However, I feel no connection with him. You and Ama took me in and raised me as your own son and, as far as I'm concerned, that is who I am, regardless of what happens today."

Ollin hugged his son tightly and said, "Now go out and fulfill your destiny."

Enough of the mushy stuff, you two, thought Tez, slightly nauseated. We need to stay focused here. First, win the match, then we can hug each other as much as we want.

As the guard entered the room to escort Matzin to the stadium, Tez was still trying to figure out how he could help Matzin beat Axolo or at least stop him from being killed.

CHAPTER THIRTY

The stadium was packed, but unlike other ball games an expectant hush had fallen over the crowd. It had been a long time since a Tlachtli match had been used as divination and the Aztec people understood the significance of the momentous event. Ama and Pica had finally found Ollin and they all sat together on a bench near the raised dais where the Emperor would soon be sitting. Ollin and Ama were thankful that everyone was too caught up in the event to notice Pica, who was sitting quietly between them, still wearing the hooded cloak.

Suddenly, four warriors entered the stadium, two holding conch shells, and two carrying drums. They walked to different corners of the ball court and began to play their instruments. Then, Teo, the priest, entered and walked to the Emperor's platform. He sat on a bench just to the right of the Emperor's throne, which had been placed on the platform earlier that day. The drums got louder as Toltec entered the stadium. He was an imposing figure in his ceremonial garb. The richly embroidered purple and gold cloak befitted a man of his importance, and his lip plug was of the finest gold. He stood on the dais and held up his hand. The music immediately stopped. Addressing the crowd, he said, "As you all know by now, the Tlachtli game today shall be used to determine the future course of our Empire. It is, therefore, a solemn occasion. There shall be no cheering for either player and there shall absolutely be no betting on the outcome. Whoever wins the match shall be deemed the successor to my throne, as ordained by the gods, and shall be so accepted by you. Is that clear?"

The crowd hesitatingly gave its assent.

Toltec continued, "Points will be given for various skills and maneuvers. But, as always, if one of the player hits the ball through a ring, he will immediately be deemed the winner even if the other player has more points. If no one hits the ball through a ring, the player with the most points at sundown will be the champion. Teo will now give the opening prayer."

Teo stood up and, facing the twin temples, said, "Gods, we, the Aztecs, implore you to reveal the future by means of this ball game. Should Axolo win, he shall be the successor to the throne and Matzin shall be banished from the kingdom forever. However, should Matzin be victorious, Matzin shall be the successor to the throne and Axolo shall remain an elite warrior. May your will be revealed to us through this game and may we accept it unquestioningly."

The frightened murmurs of the crowd made it clear that the people had heard the rumor that Matzin was an evil witch and, therefore, fervently hoped that Axolo would win. The priest sat down and Toltec commanded, "Have the players enter the arena and let the ball game begin."

Axolo entered first and Ama's heart sank. The muscles on the warrior's upper torso bulged and his expression was fierce and angry. Ollin, catching his wife's worried expression, reached across Pica and patted his wife's hand. Before Axolo took his place on the left side of the long, rectangular court, he turned to Matzin who was waiting a couple of steps behind him and said in a sneering voice, "If you want to give up now and save yourself the embarrassment of losing a ball game in record time, go right ahead."

Matzin didn't bother to reply. Just brushing flies from my

body, he repeated to himself. When it was Matzin's turn to enter, he was shocked by the hostile glares of the crowd. They must still believe I'm a witch, he thought sadly. Then, he caught sight of the loving faces of his parents and was incredibly surprised and overjoyed to see between them Pica's face peeking out from under a cloak and smiling at him. I'll make her proud of me, he vowed to himself.

The little salamander watched the two players take their positions on opposite sides of the court. He had stationed himself on the ledge of the wall encircling the court and was still racking his brain trying to think of how he could help Matzin. A warrior brought in the small, solid and heavy rubber ball and handed it to Axolo since it was the custom for the champion to start the game with the first throw. To the surprise of the spectators, Axolo didn't even try for either of the small stone rings mounted vertically at the center of the side walls. Instead, he launched the ball right at Matzin. Ama closed her eyes and Pica gasped. Matzin jumped out of the way just in time and felt the ball lightly graze his left side. "Just brushing flies away," he repeated, as he reached down to pick up the ball. As the game got under way, Matzin realized that he may not be as strong as Axolo, but practicing in the small food shed had forced him to be nimble to avoid getting hit by the ball as it ricocheted off the walls. This acquired quickness would hopefully help him avoid the balls that Axolo was intentionally throwing directly at him. Matzin picked up the ball, focused his eyes on the left ring and threw the ball with all his might. Not even close. Axolo deftly caught the ball before it hit the ground and immediately threw it back, this time trying for one of the rings. It glanced off the edge of the stone and was caught by Matzin, who slammed it across the court, missing the ring by mere inches. Axolo grabbed the ball and propelled it towards the opposite ring. It looked like it was a perfect shot. But suddenly, as if out of nowhere, Matzin's gloved hand appeared in front of the ring, skillfully catching the hard ball. Axolo cursed under his breath. This was not going to be as easy as he thought. How did Matzin learn to play like this? he wondered. But, he still was not worried. He would just wear Matzin down, like he did with all of his other opponents. Eventually he would win. He had no doubt.

****

As the sun started to sink behind the twin temples, Omo opened her eyes and stretched out her wings. She noticed that Axolo had not yet returned. He must still be at the stadium because his sports equipment is not here either, she thought to herself. This surprised her because generally the ball game matches were over long before the sun started to go down. The owl decided to fly over to the ball court, excited about having the unexpected pleasure of seeing Axolo, the champion, in action.

****

Tez grew increasingly concerned as the ball game dragged on. The elongated shadows on the court meant that it was getting late and Tez saw that Matzin was growing tired. Axolo, taking advantage of Matzin's weary state, kept trying to hit Matzin with the ball. So far, Matzin had only sustained a few minor blows to his upper thighs and forearms but Tez knew it was only a matter of time before the injuries became more severe.

The salamander was actually amazed that Matzin had lasted this long against such a formidable opponent. I guess he has what it takes to be a leader after all, Tez thought proudly. But he won't be of much use to the Aztec nation if he is crippled or killed during this stupid game. It was time to take matters into his own hands. He knew that by helping Matzin this time he risked losing his own life, but he had no choice. He had been chosen by the gods to protect this future Emperor and he intended to do just that. He scrambled off the ledge and down the interior wall of the Tlachtli court until he reached the hard ground. Everyone was so intent on the game that no one noticed the little salamander scurrying across the court towards the large warrior.

If I can climb inside Axolo's equipment I can hopefully distract him from his game long enough for Matzin to even the score with some more points of his own. It's a long shot but the only idea I have. And with the size of my brain, I'm lucky I have any ideas at all.

****

As Omo approached the stadium, she heard the ball slamming off the walls of the court but she was surprised that the spectators were so silent. She circled over the court and then perched on the back of the Emperor's throne. Toltec didn't even notice because he was so absorbed in the game.

"Sire," said Teo respectfully, "Axolo is still winning and the sun is starting to set."

"Yes," replied Toltec, "but not by as much as I would have thought. Matzin is remarkably skilled, especially given the fact that this is apparently the first time he has faced an opponent. However, within minutes the sky will be dark and the game will be over. Barring a miracle, it appears that Axolo will retain his title as champion."

"And his right to the throne," added Teo.

The Emperor nodded. After all that Axolo had accomplished, it seemed only fitting that he should be the next ruler. However, Toltec had already been forced to abandon his fifth son once. The thought of banishing Matzin and losing him again was more than he thought he could bear. Ollin, of course, would be heartbroken. But, unfortunately, Matzin's unfavorable birth sign required such drastic measures. And the gods, by allowing Axolo to win this game, were forcing his hand.

Omo was shocked by the conversation she was overhearing between the Emperor and the priest. Was it true that Axolo's succession to the throne depended on the outcome of this game? That was the problem with being a nocturnal security guard, she thought angrily. Humans seemed to make all of their important decisions during the day and reserved the night for sleeping. She was always out of the loop. Well, fortunately, Axolo appeared to be winning. And anyone could see that his opponent was hurt and tired. But then something on the court caught her predatory eye. Some sort of small animal was scurrying toward Axolo. Worried that Axolo would be distracted by the animal or trip over it, Omo instinctively sprung into action. Flying up above the court, she set her sights on the interfering animal and dove, hurtling toward the ground at a terrifying speed.

Tez didn't know what hit him. He had almost reached Axolo when suddenly he was scooped off the ground and, for the second time in his short life, found himself flying through the air.

Clutching the salamander tightly in her talons, Omo flew up and over the stadium wall. Tez, thinking that the owl intended to devour him, tried to wriggle out of her solid grip. He reasoned that if he were going to die anyway, it would be better to die immediately by falling to the ground than to be eaten alive. Little did he know, Omo had no intention of eating him. Wanting to get back to make sure that Axolo had won the ball game, her plan was to simply drop the pesky salamander far enough away from the stadium so that he wouldn't have a chance to return before the end of the match. Therefore, just as she flew over the wall encircling the temple precinct, she loosened her grip. As the salamander hurtled towards the ground, Omo executed a perfect 180-degree turn and hastened back to the ball court.

Axolo had just caught the ball in his gloved hand when the owl dove into the ball court. The crowd gasped and both players were completely thrown off guard. Axolo, however, recognizing that the intruder was none other than his lucky owl, saw the interruption as a sign from the gods that he would be the victor. Matzin, on the other hand, felt sick to his stomach. For he saw the owl pick up his little friend, the salamander. How he had gotten here, Matzin had no idea. It was as if the little creature had been making some misguided attempt to help him win the game. And now the salamander, his dear companion would end up as the evening meal for an owl.

Recognizing that Matzin was still focused on the owl, who was now flying out of the ball court, Axolo smiled malevolently. He knew the score of the game was too close for comfort and he was embarrassed that he was not decisively beating this rookie player. But the owl had fortuitously provided him with the opportunity to both win the game and take out Matzin at the same time. Knowing he had to act quickly, while Matzin was still distracted by the owl, Axolo heaved the heavy ball straight at Matzin's unprotected chest.

Pica's unmistakable scream caused Matzin to take his eyes off the owl and his prey just in time to feel the full weight of the ball slam into him and knock him to the ground. He gasped for air as a searing pain spread across his entire upper body. While writhing in agony, Matzin saw Axolo smiling and lifting up his arms victoriously. The warrior turned his back to Matzin and started walking confidently towards the platform upon which the Emperor sat. The sun had just about disappeared from the sky and many spectators stood, believing the match to be over. Ollin, Ama and Pica looked for the quickest way to get to the injured boy. The rest of the crowd, now watching the Emperor, and waiting for his pronouncement, didn't notice Matzin as he picked up the ball and slowly stood up. Nauseous, he fell back to his knees and vomited. Part of him just wanted to give up. He was so tired and so hurt. He just wanted to go home. Then, he reminded himself that if he lost this match, he would have no home. He would be banished from the Empire, far away from everyone that he loved. Axolo, the cocky, pitiless warrior would have won. Matzin would rather die. Using every ounce of strength left in his bruised and battered body, he stood up again, fighting the nausea that threatened to once more overtake him. Bringing back his arm, he focused intently on the ring attached to the right wall of the ball court. Unable to stand the pain any longer, he screamed as he released the ball. Startled by the scream, the crowd and Axolo turned back towards Matzin just in time to see the ball sail cleanly through the ring as the sun sank completely below the horizon.

"I believe that makes me the winner," Matzin whispered as he slumped to the ground in agony.

CHAPTER THIRTY ONE

The crowd was stunned. Axolo couldn't believe his eyes. Toltec stared in disbelief at the ball now lying on the ground not far from the stone ring. Axolo was the first to recover. I don't care who won the stupid game, he thought. There is no way that Matzin is going to steal the crown from me. I worked too hard for it.

Then, he had an idea. Turning to the crowd, he exclaimed, "Fellow citizens, as many of you know, there is strong evidence to suggest that my opponent is a witch." Axolo was pleased to hear murmured agreement among the spectators. "It is obvious that when my back was turned and your attention was no longer focused on him, Matzin used the evil art of witchcraft to cause the ball to go through the ring. There is no other logical explanation for what has happened. The severe blow he received from the ball I launched at him would have completely incapacitated a mere mortal. And how else to explain a novice defeating the undisputed Tlachtli champion? Is this really who you want to rule over you? A witch who had the audacity to abduct Tlaloc's sacrificial victim thereby incurring the Rain God's wrath upon our nation?"

The spectators had conflicting emotions. On the one hand, this was a game of divination. If the all-powerful gods had wanted Axolo to win, he would have won. However, allowing a witch to rule over the Aztec Empire was inconceivable. If it could be proven that Matzin had used witchcraft during the game, he would have to forfeit and Axolo would be declared the victor. Toltec had come to the same conclusion. He turned to Teo, "Is there any way to prove that Matzin used witchcraft at the end of the match?"

Listening to the increasingly vociferous crowd, and overhearing the Emperor's question, Ollin decided he had had enough. While everyone was trying to justify denying his son the victory he had fought so hard for, it was clear that Matzin needed immediate medical attention.

Standing up, he yelled out, "Fellow citizens, I have healed many of you, helped you with difficult births of your sons and daughters, and been there to ease the pain of a loved one's final moments. I have been welcomed in your homes. But today, I am ashamed of each and every one of you. You have blindly accepted and spread hateful rumors about Matzin, never bothering to seek the truth. Ama and I have raised and loved Matzin since he was an infant.

"After receiving revelations from the gods that Matzin was to be next in line to the throne, my wife and I tried to instill in our son the virtues he would need to lead our nation. Watching him perform today, I believe we have succeeded. Axolo, on the other hand, exhibited a complete lack of self-control and poor sportsmanship upon losing the game. Qualities I would neither expect nor desire from a future Emperor.

"As for the allegation that Matzin stole the Rain God's victim, it is true. But instead of cursing my son, you should be down on your knees, thankful that he acted so selflessly. You see, Matzin discovered that the victim was imperfect and knew Tlaloc would be displeased with her..."

"You're just trying to protect him," exclaimed Axolo, stung by Ollin's rebuke, "How do we know Matzin hasn't put a spell on you to make you say whatever he wants you to? It's not as if sorcerers are immune to evil spells. As for the sacrificial victim,

I found her myself. And I can state unequivocally that she was the most perfect victim this Empire has ever seen. Tlaloc would have been very pleased.'

"That is a lie!" shouted a female voice next to Ollin. Everyone turned towards the source of the voice, as Pica stood and threw off her hooded cloak. "I am the victim Axolo speaks of," she declared as the crowd gasped. "However, this careless warrior was in such a hurry to carry me off that he failed to notice the large, purple birthmark on the bottom of my right foot." Turning towards the Emperor, she said, "Sire, may I approach the platform to prove to you that I speak the truth?"

"Certainly, my child," replied Toltec, whose head was spinning with the rapid turn of events.

Guards helped Pica onto the dais. Just then, a priest, unnoticed by the crowd, whose entire attention was focused on the lovely young girl, entered the ball court, approached Teo, and whispered in his ear. Teo nodded, looking relieved. Pica turned her back to the Emperor and bent her knee.

"It is as she has said," Toltec said to the crowd. Then, turning back to Pica, he said, "But there is something I don't understand. Why on earth are you here today?"

Pica started to explain when she was rudely interrupted by Axolo.

"Father, can't you see? Witchcraft brought her here today, witchcraft made an ugly stain appear on a once unblemished foot, and witchcraft is the only thing that allowed Matzin to win this game. Therefore, I am the champion!"

"Sire, Matzin is no more a witch than I am," declared Teo from his seat behind the throne. "I have just been informed that Kan, our high priest, has passed away. As much as we all mourn this great loss, I am also relieved, because I can now fill in the missing pieces of the puzzle for you by revealing the confession

Kan made to me."

As Teo explained about Kan's irreparable mistake concerning Matzin's birth sign, Toltec's eyes filled with tears. Axolo realized that there was no hope now of being the successor to the throne. Even he wasn't capable of taking on the entire Aztec army. He stalked angrily out of the ball court, glaring resentfully at Matzin. The spectators' utterances grew louder as they struggled to digest what they had just heard. Ama found her way onto the ball court and began rubbing ointment onto Matzin's many wounds. Omo was confused by the incredible revelations. How was this possible? She had clearly been ordered by the gods to protect Axolo, who was to become the next Emperor. Had the gods changed their plans without notifying her? That was certainly their prerogative but awfully inconsiderate. Well, the owl knew one thing for sure. She had not been relieved of her duty to guard Axolo no matter what the future held for him. So, she quickly flew out of the stadium and followed overhead as Axolo walked stiffly towards the calmecac building.

****

Toltec called to one of his guards."Carry Matzin carefully to the palace. Ama and the girl will accompany you. Make sure that they are provided with everything they need."

Then, turning to the rest of the guards, he ordered them to clear the stadium, asking only that Ollin remain with him. As they exited, the spectators talked among themselves in loud whispers, knowing that what they had just witnessed would become an oft-repeated story for generations to come.

Soon the arena was empty except for the Emperor and the sorcerer.

"Ollin, you have been a good and trusted friend for as long as I can remember. Therefore, I will admit only to you that I don't think my tired, old body can withstand the jolt from everything that has happened here today. My heart has been broken so many times. I have buried three sons, abandoned my youngest son, and today, because of an unintentional mistake made years ago, was forced to watch two of my children fight for the right to wear my crown. I confess to feeling torn. On the one hand, I am overjoyed that Matzin will be able to remain in the kingdom and that I will be given the opportunity, albeit late, of getting to know this young man who shares my blood. I commend you Ollin on raising him so well. However, my heart bleeds for Axolo. I am not blind to his faults. He can be hotheaded and stubborn, but he has dedicated his life to proving himself worthy to take my place."

"May I speak frankly, Sire?"

"Of course, Ollin."

"There is nothing you could have done to change what happened today. We must accept the destiny that was chosen by the gods for both Matzin and Axolo. Now, it is up to each of them to make the most out of what he has been given. In my opinion, the greatest test of their characters lies ahead. As we have been taught for generations, 'the man who bears his honors and burdens impassively, aloof from his shifting fortunes, is the most admired,...'"

"And the man who bears his honors haughtily and his burdens resentfully shall be the most despised," Toltec said, completing the proverb each Aztec child learned by heart at an early age.

"Perhaps now would be a good time to remind Axolo of the truth contained in that saying," Ollin advised.

"As always you have told me what I needed to hear, Ollin. Why don't you return to the palace? I'm sure you are anxious about Matzin."

"Thank you, Sire. Will you be accompanying me?"

"I will be along shortly. First, I must find Axolo."

Ollin nodded, wishing that he had a magic potion to relieve the pain in his old friend's heart.

CHAPTER THIRTY TWO

No one noticed the spotted salamander climbing up the right wall of one of the many canals that dissected the capital city. His little, spotted body was battered and bruised and there was a puncture wound on his belly caused by the owl's tight grip. But, the fact that he was even alive was a miracle, and he knew it.

As he had tumbled through the air, expecting these to be his last moments on earth, he had prayed to the gods that they would choose a worthy successor to take his place as Matzin's guardian. But the gods clearly had other plans, because instead of smashing into the hard ground, Tez had splashed into the cool, refreshing waters of the canal.

"You never know when being an amphibian will come in handy," he thought to himself as he gingerly resurfaced and swam towards the canal wall. Then, he scurried back onto dry ground and headed back to the ball court. As he approached the temple precinct gates, a flood of people burst through the opening, speaking excitedly. Tez plastered himself against the wall to avoid being trampled upon.

"In your lifetime, have you ever heard of a high priest making such a costly mistake as misreading a birth sign?" Tez overheard a young man say.

"It's incredible!" replied another, "I walk into the stadium believing that Axolo's opponent is a witch, and hours later discover that he's not a witch at all, but, instead, is destined to be the next Aztec Emperor."

"And what an amazing shot he made at the end of the match. Right through the ring!"

"He was badly hurt though when they carried him off to the palace."

"With one of the finest sorcerers in the land caring for him, he should be all right...."

Tez was flabbergasted. When he had been so rudely removed from the arena, Matzin had been hurt, tired and about to lose. Now, it appeared that his young charge had won not only the game, but his right to the throne. Tez felt like someone who was reading a story where the beginning and end were both intact but the pages in-between had been removed. Well, all that matters is that all is as it should be, thought the little salamander happily. However, he never liked relying on seond-hand news, especially when it was this important. So, ignoring his painful injuries, he darted in and out of the crowd toward the palace hoping to find Matzin recovering rapidly from his wounds.

****

The Emperor entered Axolo's room and was saddened, but not surprised, to find his son stuffing his belongings into a leather knapsack.

"Axolo, we need to talk."

Axolo didn't even look up from what he was doing.

"There's nothing to talk about, Father. Matzin's in and I'm out. That was made very clear on the ball court."

"I understand that you are upset. You worked hard in the calmecac school to prepare yourself for what you believed to be your destiny. You proved yourself to be a brave, elite warrior and distinguished yourself in many battles. Nothing that happened today diminishes all that you have accomplished. However, I feel that I have perhaps failed you as a father."

For the first time, Axolo, surprised, looked up as Toltec continued.

"You see, your teachers taught you almost everything a young man needs to know to be an effective leader. But somewhere along the way, you never incorporated into your character two important things: humility and compassion. Frankly, I was embarrassed by your lack of sportsmanship on the court today."

Axolo's eyes darkened with anger. How dare he lecture me on my shortcomings after all that I have been through? he thought.

"Humility and compassion don't win battles, Sire," responded Axolo disdainfully.

"That is true. But they are very useful in negotiating terms of peace after the battle is over."

"Well, since Matzin has never set foot on a battlefield, let's hope for the sake of the nation, that his heart overflows with humility and compassion.," Axolo replied sarcastically, as he swung the bulging knapsack over his shoulder and grabbed his quiver and bow.

"Axolo," Toltec said harshly. "That is enough! If anyone else had used such a disrespectful tone with me they would have been severely punished."

"Well, why don't you banish me from the kingdom since I'm leaving anyway?" Axolo responded.

"Axolo," sighed Toltec, "I wish you would reconsider. You are one of the best warriors in the Empire and in line to be chief of the knights. That is nothing to scoff at."

"The day I bow down to Matzin as my Emperor will be the day the stars come crashing down from the heavens!"

"Son, your future path was decided when you were placed in your mother's womb. It was determined by the gods. Running away won't change anything."

"The gods have..." Axolo said in a scoffing tone. "The

gods have placed me in the palm of their hands and rolled me about like patolli dice. I've been humiliated, beaten and scarred in battle, all of which I withstood knowing the prize was worth it. But, the prize has just been stripped out of my hands and so it is time for me to carve out my own destiny in another land. Something more befitting the son of an Emperor."

"Son, I am alarmed at your blasphemous language!" Toltec exclaimed. "Deep in your heart you know that you have only one choice. Embrace your destiny and make yourself worthy of it or fight your destiny and continue to be a disappointed and angry young man."

Not bothering to respond, Axolo walked towards the door. The Emperor, realizing that nothing he had said had made any difference, watched helplessly as his son walked out the door and down the moonlit hallway. Just as Axolo started to turn the corner to exit the building, the sudden sound of flapping wings coming from the corner of the room startled the Emperor. As Toltec turned his head, he was shocked to see a large owl flying straight at him. He instinctively ducked as the large bird darted through the doorway over his head. When he looked up once more he was dismayed to find that the hallway was empty.

CHAPTER THIRTY THREE

As the sun's warm rays began to filter through the palace windows, on the day after the unforgettable ball game, Ama finally felt like she could breathe normally again. Matzin's wounds had been much more serious than she had expected and, at one point during the seemingly endless night, she and Ollin had feared that they were going to lose their son. She had been thankful to have Pica by her side assisting her in every way possible as her son fell in and out of consciousness. Now, at last, they were beginning to see some improvement in Matzin's condition. His breathing was no longer labored and his face was not so pale.

Throughout the night, the Emperor had appeared from time to time to check on Matzin and to make sure that his guests were well provided for. During one of his many visits, he gave Ollin a brief account of what had transpired between him and Axolo. Although he would never have said this to Toltec, Ollin was relieved that Axolo had decided to leave the kingdom. After seeing the pure unadulterated hatred in Axolo's eyes every time he looked at Matzin, Ollin was convinced that the two brothers could never have worked peacefully together.

Ollin's thoughts were interrupted as Toltec once more entered. The dark circles under the Emperor's eyes underscored the fact that he had not been able to get any sleep either.

"Any improvement, Ollin?" Toltec asked hopefully.

"Actually yes, Sire. I think he's over the worst of it now."

"Oh gods be praised!" exclaimed the Emperor.

Toltec's booming voice woke Matzin from a deep sleep. At first, he was disoriented by the whitewashed stone walls that surrounded him. But then, he remembered being carried to the palace. He tried to sit up but a jabbing pain in his chest caused him to quickly lie back down again. He looked up at his parents questioningly.

"Just a few broken ribs and some bad bruises. Nothing that won't heal over time if you don't try and do too much too quickly," replied Ama. "And yes, you won the match."

"Are you hungry? Thirsty?" asked Ollin.

"Yes, both," answered Matzin hoarsely, for he hadn't used his voice in a while.

Immediately, Toltec commanded a servant to bring Matzin warm turkey broth, freshly baked tortillas and water.

"Anything else we can do to make you more comfortable, Matzin?" asked the Emperor.

"No, Sire, thank you," Matzin replied softly, amazed that the Emperor was being so solicitous. After all, Matzin had just broken his son's unbeaten record on the ball court and prevented Axolo from succeeding to the throne. Nevertheless, Matzin couldn't help his eyes from glowing with satisfaction and pride as he recalled the final moments of the game and the look on Axolo's face upon being defeated.

As if reading Matzin's mind, the Emperor knelt next to the young man and held his hand.

"The outcome of the game was decided by the will of the gods. You are the rightful heir to the crown and you earned that right by the phenomenal way you played yesterday. I cannot pretend that my heart is not heavy for Axolo and the pain he is going through right now, but the gods obviously have a different path for him to follow. My one regret is that I was separated from you for so long. I know that you will always consider Ollin as your father, which is as it should be. But, I want you to know that I will always think of you as my son."

Matzin nodded, too overcome with all that had happened to respond properly. Just then, Etta burst into the room unannounced.

"Sire! Wonderful news!" Then, she stopped short and her face turned the color of her white cotton tunic. There on a mat in front of her was a boy who looked remarkably like the Empress. On his right forearm was a purple birthmark, identical to the one she had seen so many years ago on an otherwise perfect baby boy.

Toltec realized that because Etta had been keeping constant vigil at his wife's bedside she would have had no way of knowing the unbelievable events that had occurred in the past few days. He quickly supported her with his arms and guided her to the wall where he gently set her down.

"I don't understand..." she stammered. "What has happened? Is this who I think it is?"

"I'll explain everything, Etta. Don't worry," replied the Emperor. "But first, what brought you here? I hope that you have not left my wife unattended."

Etta struggled to regain her composure. She was so shocked by what she was seeing that the old woman was having trouble remembering what she was doing there. Then, upon hearing Toltec say "my wife," it all came flooding back.

"Sire, your wife has awakened from her coma. She is asking for you."

Toltec's face lit with pleasure and he started to stride happily out of the room when all of a sudden he stopped short. His face filled with despair.

"What's troubling you, Sire?" asked Etta, understandably surprised at the Emperor's bizarre reaction to such good news.

As if he didn't even hear the old woman, Toltec turned towards Ollin and asked, "What do I do?"

Ollin knew immediately what was troubling his old friend.

"You will eventually have to tell Mia the truth," responded Ollin. "But right now her health is too precarious. Frankly, it is a miracle she has come back to us at all. For several weeks at least, you must make sure that she remains completely oblivious to these events."

"And then?"

'And then, slowly, over time, you will tell her everything that has happened."

"What if the shock of it all makes her sick again?"

"It's always a possibility. But eventually she will hear the news anyway. It's all anyone is talking about. Better that she hears it in a loving, gentle manner from you than from a stranger's casual remarks in the marketplace."

Etta's head was spinning.

"Sire, can someone please tell me what's going on?" she asked.

"Walk with me to my wife's chambers and I will do my best to bring you up to date," replied Toltec. "Then, perhaps between the two of us we can think of the best way to reveal the news to Mia."

He helped the old faithful woman into a standing position and then, together, they left the room. Moments later, a servant entered holding a tray laden with food and drink.

"Should I roll up some blankets to place beneath Matzin's head so that it's easier for him to eat?" asked a voice.

"That would be very helpful, Pica. Thank you," replied Ama.

Pica, who had been sitting quietly in the corner, unnoticed by Matzin, crossed the room and grabbed some folded blankets that had been stacked next to the doorway. Matzin's eyes followed her every movement. She was so graceful and beautiful. He had no idea why she was here but he was glad that she was. As Pica handed the blankets to the sorceress, she said shyly, "Matzin, we were all so worried about you. Most people would not have recovered from the blows you received yesterday. It is such a relief to see you feeling better."

"Thanks," Matzin replied, longing to say something else to her but unable to think of anything clever.

After her son had finished his soup and the last bite of tortilla, Ama smiled with satisfaction and declared, "Anyone that can eat that heartily will soon fully recover." Then, turning to the young girl, she added, "Pica, you have been so helpful these past couple of days. And now that my son is out of danger it is time for me to belatedly keep the promise I made to return you to your village."

Pica's face lit up with joy. Matzin, however, suddenly felt like the meal he had just devoured had turned into a large piece of volcanic rock that was sitting in the pit of his stomach.

"Why don't you let me take her back, love?" suggested Ollin. "I have patients in the outerlying areas of the city that I need to see anyway."

"All right. I'll stay here and make sure that 'the future Emperor' gets back on his feet as quickly as possible."

Matzin wished that he were already back on his feet. Then, he could have traveled back with Pica himself. Ollin squeezed his son's shoulder affectionately, kissed Ama's cheek and then picked up the leather pouch that contained his healing potions. But as the sorcerer and Pica started to leave the room, Matzin blurted out, "Wait!" Startled, they both turned towards him questioningly.

"What is it, son?" asked Ollin.

Embarassed by his outburst, Matzin stammered, "Nothing really... I mean, well, would it be possible Pica for me to... I mean could I sometime...visit you?"

Pica blushed and replied with downcast eyes, "I am sure my family would be honored to meet and welcome the person who saved my life."

"Great!...I mean thanks..." responded Matzin with a

giddy grin.

Better than any medicine I could have given him, thought Ama smiling. Tez, on the other hand, who had finally reached the palace and was resting in the corner of Matzin's room, realized he would never understand humans. Yesterday, his charge had brilliantly defeated Axolo, the champion, in a game in which Matzin had never before even faced an opponent. And today, he was a stammering idiot in front of a young girl. The Aztecs better hope that when Matzin becomes their leader they continue to face armies of men; otherwise, he feared for the future of the Empire.

The little salamander had been so relieved to find that Matzin was not mortally injured. However, Tez couldn't say the same for himself. The puncture wound in his underbelly caused by the owl's talons was still quite painful and did not seem to be healing properly. It didn't help that he hadn't had a decent meal in days. He felt so tired and beaten up. His little legs felt like they could no longer carry him anywhere.

Matzin watched Ollin and Pica exit the room. With the blankets under his head he could finally see the whole room instead of just the ceiling. Suddenly, a slight movement in the corner caught his eye. Staring in disbelief, he realized that it was his little companion, the salamander.

"Boy, am I surprised to see you, little fellow!" Matzin exclaimed happily. "When that owl swooped down and gathered you up, I thought you were a goner."

Ama rushed to Matzin's side believing that he had taken a turn for the worse and was hallucinating.

"Mother, I'm fine," her son reassured her. "Do you see that salamander over there? For some reason, he has been following me around and keeping me company ever since I was a young boy. Strange, isn't it?"

"How in the world could you possibly know that it is the same creature each time?" Ama asked, still concerned that Matzin might be delirious.

"He has a unique pattern on his back. Bring him over here and I'll show you. But be careful, don't frighten him."

Ama cautiously approached the salamander and was at first surprised that it didn't scurry away. Then, she saw the festering wound and the deep scratches on its body and realized the animal was too hurt to escape. She carefully picked up the small amphibian and carried it over to her son.

"He's badly hurt, Matzin. Hold him while I mix a poultice to place on his wounds."

Tez felt safe and warm in Matzin's hands.

"You'll be all right, little friend," Matzin whispered confidently as Ama gently rubbed the mixture onto Tez's torso.

And so will you, thought Tez contentedly, thanks to me.

****

EPILOGUE

The small brown-haired girl sat on the roof of her home and clutched her mother's hand. Down below, her father and older brother were destroying all of their possessions and piling the refuse next to their house. She had just watched her brother rip her favorite cloak to shreds and her little fists clenched tightly as she tried not to cry.

The mother knew that her young daughter was frightened. And she had to admit that she was too. The New Fire Ceremony was being conducted high on the mountaintop and the fate of the Aztec people rested in its successful completion. Soon they would know whether the Sun God had decided to allow this world to continue spinning for another 52 years, or whether eternal darkness would reign over the land and the age of the Fifth Sun would be over for good. The possibility that this could potentially be her family's last night together was too awful to contemplate. The mother pulled her daughter onto her lap and kissed the top of her head. The little girl looked up and said plaintively, "Mommy, I'm scared. It's so dark and cold up here and I'm hungry."

"I know you are sweetheart. Would it help if I told you a story while we wait?"

"Oh yes, please."

"How about the story of how Emperor Matzin ended up becoming the leader of the Aztecs?"

"Yes, yes! I like that one!" replied the little girl, clapping her hands together.

The mother stroked her daughter's silky hair as she began, "Once upon a time, Kan, the high priest, was meticulously sweeping the red-ochre temple...."

****

"The book has come to an end
Your heart is now complete."
Anonymous Aztec poet

ABOUT THE AUTHOR

K.S. Miranda has had many careers, all of which she has enjoyed: an attorney specializing in real estate and environmental law, a French teacher, and a mother of incredible children. She has always had a passion for writing, and when that passion coincided with her burgeoning interest in the Aztec culture, this book was born.

Made in the USA
San Bernardino, CA
08 October 2013